Praise for *Hard*

"In Yoshimoto's world, regret becomes a fugue state with its own circadian rhythms."
—John Freeman, *Time Out New York*

"The author's trademark blend of traditional Japanese philosophical concerns and plain contemporary prose . . . Yoshimoto makes every word count. . . . [A book] warmed by the simple expressions of human emotion that make this author's work special." —*Kirkus Reviews*

"Like twins whose paths diverge dramatically, these two gentle stories share little beyond the mesmerizing voice of their creator. . . . Yoshimoto takes a subtle, graceful look at the relationship between the sisters and the fault lines in this grieving family. . . . Downright moving."
—*Publishers Weekly*

Praise for Banana Yoshimoto:

"Fans of Haruki Murakami will find a kindred spirit in Yoshimoto. . . . It would be equally reasonable to compare her to such diverse talents as Anne Tyler and Douglas Coupland. . . . Yoshimoto brings to the table compelling characters, a spare and ethereal manner of writing, and an eye for the way in which terrible experiences shape one's life." —*BookPage*

"Ms. Yoshimoto's writing is lucid, earnest and disarming, as emotionally observant as Jane Smiley's, as fluently readable as Anne Tyler's. . . . [It] seizes hold of the reader's sympathy and refuses to let go. . . . She has a wonderful tactile ability to convey a mood or sensation through her descriptions of light and sound and touch, as well as an effortless ability to penetrate her characters' hearts."   —Michiko Kakutani, *The New York Times*

"[Yoshimoto's] voice is so candid and casual, it can seem like a diary entry or a stream of consciousness monologue. . . . But the light, careless tone is deceptive. Yoshimoto's words are considered, and each of them has the weight of a small, perfectly round stone dropped into a still pool."   —*San Francisco Chronicle*

"The moods she evokes so ingenuously stick in your mind. . . . There is no such thing as a stock character in Yoshimoto's fiction. . . . Banana Yoshimoto writes utterly without pretense."
                              —*The Washington Post Book World*

HARDBOILED
&
HARD LUCK

Also by Banana Yoshimoto:

Kitchen
N. P.
Lizard
Amrita
Asleep
Goodbye Tsugumi

HARDBOILED
&
HARD LUCK

Banana Yoshimoto

Translated from the Japanese
by Michael Emmerich

Grove Press
New York

First published in Japan by Rockin' On, Inc.
English translation rights arranged through Japan Foreign-Rights Centre/
Writers House LLC.

Published simultaneously in Canada
Printed in the United States of America

Library of Congress Cataloging-in-Publication Data
Yoshimoto, Banana, 1964–

    [Hadoboirudo. English]
    Hardboiled ; & Hard luck / Banana Yoshimoto ; translated from the
Japanese by Michael Emmerich.
    p. cm.
    ISBN-10: 0-8021-4262-1
    ISBN-13: 978-0-8021-4262-7
    I. Emmerich, Michael. II. Yoshimoto, Banana, 1964– Hado rakku.
English. III. Title: Hard luck. IV. Title.
PL865.O7138H3313 2005
895.6'35—dc22   2005040210

Grove Press
an imprint of Grove Atlantic
154 West 14th Street
New York, NY 10011

Distributed by Publishers Group West

www.groveatlantic.com

23 24 25   10 9 8 7 6 5

Contents

HARDBOILED

1
The Shrine

I was traveling alone, no destination in mind.

One afternoon, I found myself walking on a mountain road.

It was the first road up the mountainside after the highway; I liked how it felt to be walking there, hidden under its lush canopy of green.

When I first set out along the road, I'd been gazing down at the lovely patterns formed by the play of shadow and light.

My heart was light then; I felt like someone starting out on a walk.

Looking at the map, I saw that the road was marked as a hiking trail, and that it would eventually rejoin the highway.

I strolled along, feeling fine, under an afternoon sun so warm it seemed like spring.

But the road was unexpectedly difficult, with lots of steep slopes.

I kept walking, throwing my heart into the task, as the sun slowly began to sink; by the time I noticed the evening star it was already gleaming in the brilliant indigo sky, its light as clear as a jewel's. To the west, in a sky still tinted with traces of pink, the long, thin, late-autumn clouds, dyed in soft colors, were gradually being swallowed up by the darkness. The moon had risen. It was a small sliver of a moon, no wider than a fingernail.

"If I keep going at this rate," I muttered to myself, "who knows when I'll reach the town."

I had been walking along in silence for so long, I had almost forgotten what my own voice sounded like. My knees were tired; my toes were beginning to ache.

"Good thing I went with the hotel. I'd be too late for dinner at an inn."

I thought about calling ahead, but I was so deep in the mountains that I couldn't use my cell phone. All of a sudden, I felt hungry. It wouldn't be that much longer until I arrived at the small town where I had reserved a room. As soon as I get there, I'll go and have a hot meal, I thought, slightly quickening my pace.

Suddenly, just as I came to a bend in the road that led back into a slightly more remote part of the mountain, beyond the reach of the streetlights, I was overcome by an extremely unpleasant sensation. I had the illusion that space itself had bent gelatinously out of shape, so that no matter how long I walked, I would never make any progress.

I've never had any sort of supernatural powers. But at a certain point I learned to sense things, even if only faintly, that my eyes can't see.

I'm a woman. Once, just once, I went out with another woman. She could see things other people couldn't. Maybe it rubbed off on me, or maybe being with her sharpened an instinct that I had

always had, I don't know. All I know is that sometime after we started living together, I began to notice when there was something·odd in the air.

A few years ago, during a car trip, on a
mountain road just like this one, she and I parted
forever. That day I was driving. If we aren't going
back to the same house, I'd rather travel on my
own for a while before I return, so just let me out
here, she begged. And she meant it. Now I know
why you packed so much, I said. I realized that
she had never intended to go home with me; she
had made up her mind even before we left. For me
to move out of her apartment was, in her eyes, a
betrayal even more serious than I had imagined.
I tried and tried to make her change her mind, but
she remained firm. She was so determined I actually thought she might kill me if I didn't do what
she wanted.

She said:

I really, really don't want to be there when
you leave. I'll take my time going home; you go on
ahead. Just have your things out by the time I get
back.

So that's what I did. Even though it was her car.

The look on her face when we said goodbye. Her lonely eyes, the way her hair hung down over her face. The beige of her coat reflected forever in the rearview mirror. It looked as if she were about to be swallowed by the green that engulfed the mountain. She kept waving, forever. I had the feeling that she would always be there waiting for me.

Things that don't matter at all to one person can hurt another so deeply it seems as bad as dying. True, I didn't know all that much about her life. But I couldn't understand why it would be so painful for her to watch someone pack up and leave her apartment. Maybe we just didn't understand each other, I don't know. It's true that I'd had nowhere to live, that I used her. And the fact is, I never planned to stay with her, a woman like myself, for the long haul. We were living together, and she liked me. So when she got physical, I responded. That's all there was to it. But before long, I realized that she saw things differently. Or rather, some part of me realized it, and I kept pretending

I hadn't noticed. I felt horrible about what I had done. She was still there inside me now, just as she always was: a life put on hold, a memory I didn't know how to handle.

My memories solidified into a mass of any number of different images and cast a relentless shadow on my heart.

I glanced up at the road ahead, trying hard to pull myself together, to focus on the rigors of the hike. And there it was, right there in front of me: that mysterious shrine. There was no statue of Jizō, the guardian of children, nor of any one of the other figures one might expect to find in his place; there was nothing but the shrine itself and offerings of flowers, long chains of origami cranes, and sake—none of which had been set out recently. A thought rose in my mind before I could stop it.

Something incredibly evil is resting here—something that used to live in the vicinity. I'm sure of it.

I can't explain why I felt this way. Maybe there used to be a statue of Jizō or something here, but it broke—maybe that's all it was? Or maybe someone carried it off? I tried to believe this. But it wasn't true. Something hung in the air there, without a doubt——a passion of terrible intensity that had kept accumulating new layers over the years until it became one dense mass. The feeling that came over me then was so creepy that I just stood and stared.

As I looked more closely, I noticed ten or so pitch-black stones, each shaped like a small egg, that had been arranged in a circle right in the middle of the shrine. There was something very eerie about them too.

I got out of there quick, trying as much as possible to keep the ring of stones out of my view. During my travels, I had sometimes come across such things. There are, without a doubt, places in this world where something has settled, and it's best for us little humans not to get involved.

I thought of various places I had visited in the past: caves I had seen in Bali and Malaysia that were so deep they made me shudder; sites in Cambodia and Saipan that brimmed with achingly dark passions left over from the war. I had visited many such places when I was young, accompanying my father on business trips—maybe that was another reason I became as sensitive to these things as I did. And it's true, when I ask about places where I've felt that something is wrong, they usually turn out to have borne witness to something terrible.

Ultimately, though, it's living people that frighten me the most. It's always seemed to me that nothing could be scarier than a person, because as dreadful as places can be, they're still just places; and no matter how awful ghosts might seem, they're just dead people. I always thought that the most terrifying things anyone could ever think up were the things living people came up with.

As I rounded the bend, the eerie feeling I'd had suddenly slipped away, drawing back from the area around my shoulders, and I found myself surrounded once more by the sounds and sensations of a quiet evening.

Night lowered its heavy curtain. The entire area was flooded with air so clear it made me feel wonderful. When a breeze blew up, fallen autumn leaves of all different colors danced up through the dusk, fluttering toward me. I felt as if I were wrapped in a piece of cloth woven in some beautiful dream.

So I forgot my fear altogether, and walked on.

After a while, the slope evened out into a gentle decline and the road widened. No sooner had I noticed the lights shining through the silhouettes of trees than I found myself arriving, all at once, in that small town. Little stores lined both sides of the street; the train station, which had ticket machines but no stationmaster, was flooded with light; and while hardly a soul was out and about, the houses were lit up.

The tavern was already packed with local men who had gathered to have a good time after work, so it would have been awkward for me to barge in. I decided to go into a run-down shop that sold *udon*.

The owner was just about to close up and seemed extremely annoyed to see me, but he grudgingly told me to come in, so I did. I was worn out from walking, and dying to sit down.

It was a small establishment: there were only four tables set out on the concrete floor. On my table stood an empty shaker labeled "Seven-Spice Hot Pepper" that looked as if it had probably been empty for about a century.

The man boiled the noodles in an offhand manner, then set the bowl before me. There you go, he said. The sounds of the variety show on TV echoed through the shop, but this only heightened the loneliness of the place. The noodles were so wretched I shuddered at the thought of eating them, and when I tried to order a beer the man told me he didn't have any. Considering how bad this place is, I'd have been better off eating at the hotel restaurant, even though it's sure to be overpriced and not very good, I thought.

The man was waiting for me to finish eating, fidgeting all the while . . . on the other hand, the noodles tasted terrible and they were barely even warm, and to top it all off, they had gotten so mushy they were falling apart. . . . I had a hard time getting them down. Thinking it might brighten my mood to check and see where my hotel was, I stuck my hand into my pocket and pulled out the map. As I withdrew my hand, I heard something fall to the floor with a clonk.

An icy chill ran through me, piercing right to the bottom of my heart.

Lying on the floor was a black, egg-shaped stone just like the ones I had seen at that creepy shrine.

No way, it can't be one of those, it's just a co-incidence. I tried to believe this, but I couldn't. I tried to tell myself that the sight of those stones had frightened me so much that I blanked out for a second and put one in my pocket without remembering. But I didn't believe this either. If I had done something like that, I would have feared for my sanity, of course, but that would have been a lot better than what I was feeling now.

I stared at the stone for a while in a kind of trance, then decided to forget the whole thing and leave it where it was, there on the floor of this nasty shop. Stop following me, I thought. Please.

The cool, collected part of my mind kept telling me there was no way a stone could have just walked into my pocket; it had probably just slipped in earlier, while I was eating my lunch outside. Either way, I decided not to think too deeply about it.

I wanted to get to the hotel as soon as possible; I wanted to be in a room of my own. I yearned to do ordinary things in an ordinary way, to watch TV, wash my hair, have some tea. The description of the hotel said it had a bath fed by hot springs. Yes, I would go stretch out in the hot water. . . .

The man had started sweeping the shop, so I stood up, leaving the rest of my *udon* uneaten. The last thing I saw as I walked out was the man's broom sending the stone skittering over toward one of the walls.

2
The Hotel

The lights were already out at the front desk. The carpet in the lobby looked a bit grubby and smelled like mold. But I was used to staying in places like this, so it didn't bother me. I was just thrilled to have arrived.

I rang the bell several times, and eventually a woman emerged from the room behind the desk— a Japanese-style room with *shōji* screens and a *tatami* floor. She was thin, somewhere in her mid-fifties, and her eyes were very sharp.

At first the woman looked as if she wanted to ask me why I was so late, but as soon as I told her I hadn't eaten, she became very friendly.

The restaurant's open till ten, she told me, so if you go in right now you'll still have time to eat. I'll explain the situation and ask them to keep the kitchen open if you want to run up and put your bag in your room—just promise me that you'll come right back down. There's only one ramen shop around here, you know, and it's closed today.

I'll be down right away, I said, and went up to my room.

I put down my bag, peeled off my smelly socks, then rushed back downstairs.

Naturally, I was the only customer in the dimly lit restaurant. A fake orchid stood in an odd vase on my table. The thick corn soup that came first, ladled into a floral-patterned bowl, tasted—surprise, surprise—like it had come from a can. What could have led us Japanese to misinterpret these things—potage and artificial flowers—as the standard accoutrements of elegance? Still, the soup, the crusty bread, and the small bottle of beer did finally warm me up.

Through the window, I could see dark mountains and a dark town. The streetlights stretched off into the distance, pinpoints of illumination. I felt as if this place I had come to was nowhere. As if I no longer had a home to return to. That road I had been on didn't lead anywhere, this trip would never end—it seemed to me as if next morning would never arrive. It occurred to me that this must be how it feels to be a ghost. Perhaps ghosts are trapped forever in a time like this, I mused. Why am I thinking about how ghosts feel, anyway? I couldn't say. No doubt I was just tired.

Glancing back out the window, I noticed a faint glow in the sky. Just at that moment, a fire engine and an ambulance zoomed by outside the hotel window. An uncanny sensation came over me, and I stood up and went to pay the bill.

I returned to my room for the thin cotton kimono the hotel provided and then headed for the spring-fed baths. When I passed the front desk, the woman I had spoken with earlier had just come in from outside, looking cold.

"Has something happened?" I asked.

"Apparently there's been a fire at the *udon* shop," said the woman.

Uh-oh, I thought.

"Did anyone die?"

The woman looked at me long and hard, not saying a word.

"You see, I had *udon* earlier," I went on. "I mean, I left without being able to finish it. I was just wondering if it was the same place."

"I thought you said you hadn't . . . oh, I see. The food there is terrible, isn't it?" said the woman. "I don't suppose anyone from the city would like it, seeing as even the locals don't eat there. I understand."

Good job, I thought. The woman had saved me from having to say something I'd rather not. After all, having a fire was bad enough.

"Don't worry, nobody died. There's just the one man who works there, and they said he managed to get out OK. Apparently he forgot to turn off the stove. It doesn't seem to have been much of a fire." The woman smiled. "Don't worry, it's not your fault, right? Go take your bath."

Who knows, maybe it *was* my fault, I thought. It's just a feeling, but . . .

I headed for the baths. To tell the truth, I was ready to get away from all this. To go to another town, to slip ahead into some time other than today. But it was too late for that now, I was already up to my neck in this night, submerged in this strange and lonely atmosphere. Already, I had the feeling that I was seeing everything through some sort of filter, and so I couldn't think seriously about anything. This night had me in its power.

The old tiles in the small spring-fed bath were decorated with a lovely design. Gazing at the pattern as it shimmered under the water, I began to feel more relaxed.

The bath was hot. I felt its heat seeping into the exhaustion of my body, the pain in my feet. I took my time washing myself in the light of the fluorescent lamp overhead.

I wished the morning would come quickly. I yearned to bask in the bright rays of the morning sun, which would wash everything away—to be enveloped in light as I now was in this water. Because I knew that for the time being I had no choice—I had to live in this night—I was like someone so sick with fever that she can't remember what it feels like to be healthy.

My face felt flushed, so I opened the window. Outside, it was dark and utterly still; the stars glittered coldly in the sky. The trees held their branches out without moving them, as if they were tangled in a darkness so thick it was palpable. Time had come to a standstill.

This is how it used to feel when I was with Chizuru.

Why am I thinking about her so much today? I wondered.

I looked down at my naked body. White legs and a white stomach, just the same as always, and the curves of my nails. Then, all of a sudden, it hit me. Today was the anniversary of her death.

I wished upon a small star that her soul was at peace.

May the gods accept her as she is—her good points, her rare and special nature, the sense of frailty that hung about her. Let her have an especially soft bed with a canopy overhead. Give her the sweetest heavenly sake to drink. And let her be reborn into an especially easy life. You can even take a year off my life if you have to, since it looks like I'll be around for a while anyway. Please, I'm begging you.

Somehow this made me feel better. And so, thoroughly warmed by my bath, I returned to my room.

3
A Dream

The fatigue I had felt earlier was much worse after my bath, and I made matters worse by drinking a small bottle of sake from the hotel fridge. I tumbled into bed almost immediately. Without unpacking my bag, still wearing the hotel kimono, even forgetting to switch off the bedside lamp, I entered the world of sleep. There was nothing in the room but a bed, and nothing visible from the window but the mountains behind the hotel. When I open my eyes, I thought as I sank into sleep, the morning sun will be glowing through the sun-bleached curtains, streaming into the room. And by then, the rather eerie experience I had today will be a thing of the past. . . . This thought, which flitted through my mind immediately before I fell asleep, made me breathe a sigh of relief.

But the world wasn't that friendly.

Time expands and contracts. When it expands, it's like pitch: it folds people in its arms and holds them forever in its embrace. It doesn't let us go very easily. Sometimes you go back again to the place you've just come from, stop and close your eyes, and realize that not a second has passed, and time just leaves you there, stranded, in the darkness.

In my dream, I was in a sort of maze.

I crept forward on my hands and knees through a darkness crisscrossed with narrow passageways. Tunnels kept splitting off in different directions. I tried to keep calm as I considered the options, tried to focus on finding my way back out. Every so often I would come to a place tall enough that I could stand up, but from there the path would just divide again and keep going.

Finally I saw light ahead. I pressed on.

Moving into the brightness, I discovered a small cave hung with many different colored strips of cloth and filled with burning candles. Peering through the fabric, I saw a shrine. Hold on, I thought, I know this shrine. In my dream, I realized that I had seen it before.

Just then, someone whispered in my ear, "Don't you remember the date? It's the ——th of the ——th month." I could barely make out the words, but the sound of them still gave me an unpleasant feeling. It was a day I wanted to forget. Yes . . . I think this was that sort of day.

A scene came to mind. I saw a room, one I remembered very well. The highway that ran past the building was visible through the window, and it was always very noisy, and you could smell the exhaust from the cars. The floor of the room was dirty and the walls were thin. I was living there, living with someone. . . .

At this point, I noticed a shadow flickering in the candlelight.

"You have to make an offering," said Chizuru.

That's right, I thought in my dream, it was her.

She must have been following me for some time and entered the cave behind me. She looked just as she always had: the same fair skin, the shortly cropped hair, the same lonely look on her face.

Without so much as a glance in my direction, she began making a line of black stones on a platform that seemed to serve as an altar.

"I collected these stones from the riverbed," said Chizuru.

I felt that I needed to reply.

"I guess you mean *that* river, right?" I said. "The one that separates the land of the living from the land of the dead? No living person can go there, huh?"

This was all I could manage, even at a time like this? I couldn't believe myself.

"That's right," replied Chizuru, without looking at me. "I thought I'd make an offering. After all, today *is* the anniversary of my death."

"Shouldn't I be doing that?" I said.

"Yeah, right—except you forgot." Chizuru laughed. "You were strolling along there in the mountains, totally oblivious, humming as you went."

I didn't know what to say to this.

"You still don't get it, do you?" she continued. "You always think your own life is the hardest, and as long as you get along OK, as long as life is nice and easy and you're having all the fun you can, everything's just fine."

Chizuru's eyes smoldered with a rage darker than any I had ever seen. I felt a deep hurt and anger at the unfairness of what she was saying. I had always loved Chizuru, in my own way.

"Yeah, if only my problems were more serious, right? Because compared to yours, the misfortunes I've borne are nothing at all, are they? Compared to all the big problems you had, my life is just as easy as can be, isn't it! I couldn't even win the consolation prize in a singing contest, because I couldn't inspire enough pity!"

My voice trembled with an anger I couldn't restrain. But even as I spoke, I was thunderstruck to notice that I really did tend to think my life was extremely hard, much more than I had previously realized.

It was hot in the cave, and the air was thin. I really wish there were a window, I thought. How long will I be here? The candles cast a dim glow on the dirt walls. The scent of dust and mold hung in the air.

It was so hot that I woke up. Light streamed across the ceiling. I was bathed in sweat, and my head was throbbing from the pressure of the dream. My kimono was twisted uncomfortably around my body, and the sheets were tangled. God, I thought, what an awful dream.

I glanced at the clock: it was two in the morning. I was wide awake now, and I didn't think I'd be able to go back to sleep. I got out of bed, took a bottle of water from the fridge, and drank. Gulped the water down. It was only at that moment that I began, finally, to feel alive. No wonder I'm hot, I thought, noticing that the heat was on—the thermostat was set too high. I rotated the dial on the ancient machine and adjusted the temperature.

It was late. The room was deathly still; nothing moved.

I got up and looked out the window. It was pitch-black, and there was no sign of movement out there either. My own face was reflected in the glass.

It's no good, I thought. Something just doesn't feel right tonight.

I guess I did pick up something on the road, after all. This mood.

The Chizuru I had encountered in my dream didn't convey the same feeling of depth as the real Chizuru. She had seemed thin, insubstantial. It was a dream, I told myself, just a dream.

Chizuru wasn't the sort of person who said things like that. She was stronger, more forbidding, and more bitterly sarcastic; she was also much cleverer, and nicer. Clearly the Chizuru I dreamed was a product of my own feelings of guilt.

After I lay down for a while, I began to get sleepy again.

The next thing I knew, I was back in the cave. Here we go again, I thought.

Chizuru was kneeling with her eyes closed, praying with all her heart. She was beautiful. The walls of the cave were gray in the candlelight. Chizuru looked so dignified, she made the cave seem as if it had been created just for prayer.

In the wavering light, her eyelashes took on an air of fragility. Her eyes—those beautifully cold brown eyes of hers—quivered beneath closed eyelids. What was she praying for? What had caused her such suffering?

Now that I was thinking seriously, I suddenly realized that I didn't know the first thing about Chizuru. Back in those days, I didn't have a solid grasp of things, even in my own mind. I was tired, I was hurt, I was still just a kid. Looking back, it seemed as if the sky outside my window was always full of clouds. And not just clouds, either—there was a lot of fog that year, too. Night after night, the landscape outside my window was a dirty, ashy gray.

This region calls out to something in my mind, and my mind answers back—that's why I keep finding myself in this sad dream. So I might as well just enjoy seeing Chizuru again.

Because as long as she didn't speak, the Chizuru before me looked like the one I had known, and it was good to see her. That white cardigan with the frayed cuffs; the jeans whose cost we had split and then fought over until finally we agreed that whoever got up first each morning could wear them; her light brown hair with its dried-out ends—these were things I would never have a chance to see anymore, no matter how much I wanted to. I gazed at her, long and hard.

In all probability, I thought, my thoughts had never gotten through to her, not even once. This is how she always was, sunk in the depths of her own inner life. She didn't even try to make others understand.

And I had just looked on. In fact, that was why I liked watching her. Her life was like a pale shadow of life, given form by innumerable layers of anguish.

When Chizuru turned to look at me, the candles went out, and everything was plunged in darkness.

Ah, I must have slept again. . . .

I thought.

I fell asleep and entered that dream again.

It was three o'clock. My mouth was dry, my head ached dully.

I looked around the unfamiliar room. Nothing seemed real. I pressed my face to the sheets, but they didn't feel real either. Should I have a drink? Deciding that I should, I got a bottle of whiskey from the fridge and poured myself a glass. Who cares how many times I have this dream? It doesn't matter if it's just an evil effect brought about by the place I'm in, I should be happy that I got to see

Chizuru on the anniversary of her death, even if it wasn't real. . . . I wonder where the cave is, though. Then something occurred to me: the evil person or thing or whatever it is that's responsible must have been buried alive in a cave near that shrine I saw earlier! I can't say how I knew this, but I did. Things were falling into place.

Why did I feel so certain? I didn't know, but I felt sure I was right.

I never shed a tear over Chizuru's death. Why not? And why was I so harsh with her earlier, in the dream? I should have been nicer, even if it meant lying to myself.

4
The Visitor

Just then, there was a knock at the door.

It gave me a start, but I fought down the slight fear I felt and peered out through the peephole. I thought it might be the woman from the front desk.

But the person I saw standing in the eerily bright hallway was a woman I didn't recognize, dressed in a bathrobe; she stood perfectly straight, her hands hanging at her sides, and she was all alone.

I opened the door.

"As you can see, I'm a woman," I said. "I don't hire prostitutes."

The woman replied, keeping her voice down, "Don't worry, that's not why I'm here. I've been shut out of my room."

"The person inside won't let you back in?"

"He seems to be asleep."

"You can call from my room, if you want."

"Thank you."

The woman was slender and she had long hair. The lower half of her face was particularly gaunt; she had very thin lips, but they lent her a kind of graceful air. I was stunned to catch a glimpse of hair under her bathrobe as she cut across the room—apart from the robe, she was completely naked. My god, I wondered, how long has she been standing out in the hall like that?

She was standing by the phone now, but she wasn't calling.

"You haven't forgotten your room number, have you?" I asked.

"Oh no, that's not it at all!" The woman gave her head an exaggerated shake. "The truth is, we had a fight. Even if I called, I doubt he'd answer."

"He must be feeling bad right now, though,

don't you think?" I said. "I mean, after kicking you out dressed like that . . ."

"OK, I'll just wait ten minutes and then call," she replied. "Would you mind letting me stay here, just a little while?"

I poured another glass of whiskey and offered it to her.

She held out her thin, bare arm to accept it, then took a sip.

"Have you ever had something like this happen to you?" she asked. "I mean, someone doing something terrible to you, or you doing something terrible to someone else?"

"Many times. When things head in that direction . . ." I replied. Like earlier, when I couldn't be nice to Chizuru, even in a dream. "I don't know, it's like I'm in some other world or something, that's how it is with me. I lose the ability to make ordinary decisions, and my body moves on its own."

"I know what you mean. It's like being in a bad dream," she said. "The man I'm here with has a wife, and he refuses to break up with her."

"So you quarreled, and he chased you out into the hall, naked?"

"I think he gets more violent because he knows it's his own fault. In a town as small as this, just raising your voice in public is enough to get everyone talking, so sometimes I try to pick a fight with him out on the street. He holds things in, never raises his voice or anything, but I just keep shouting. In shops, on the sidewalk, wherever. And the thing is, I can feel that I'm gradually falling into a very peculiar emotional state. It's like I'm in a plastic bag, slowly running out of oxygen. Like no one cares what I do anymore, and now it's too late, there's no going back. And then, as soon as we get into our room at the hotel, he starts hitting me. We just keep going through the same cycle, and it's really worn me down. Earlier, we were up on this road in the mountains. We started shouting at each other again, and as we walked along, I started to feel like I didn't care anymore, nothing mattered. People are already beginning to talk, and my mother thinks I should be institutionalized . . . I don't suppose I'll be able to stay in this town much longer. However you look at it, it's all over now."

She spoke very quietly, almost as if she were talking about someone else.

"I don't mean to be rude," I said, "but just having you here in my room wears me out." It was the truth. Somehow when I looked at her, when I listened to her talking, my mind seemed to go numb, and I felt as if something inside me were being sucked out. "Why don't you give him a call."

"I don't want to," she said, "not yet. I'm afraid."

"All right, then, why don't I go down, wake up the woman at the front desk, and get you another key? How would that be?"

I figured I could do that much for her.

"Yes, that seems best. Would you mind?"

"No problem at all."

"Let's talk a little more, though, OK? I need to calm down."

"Sure."

"What was it like when you were in this situation? Being with someone you constantly fought with, tooth and nail?" As she spoke, her eyes met mine. But she was so absorbed in her own affairs that her gaze didn't register anything.

"I'm sorry, I can't really say anything about that. I've never had an experience like that," I said. "In my case, things always had a touch of humor, and we had some good times, and beautiful moments—there was always something good."

That was an incredible year.

My father, who had been having an affair and hadn't been home in ages, died, secretly leaving everything to me. My mother wanted what little he'd had, so she cooked up all sorts of cunning plots, and finally made off with my personal seal and my bank passbook.

I call her my mom because she brought me up, but she isn't my biological mother. We were on pretty good terms, though, so I was really shocked by what she did. The rumor was that she had quit her job at the snack bar where she used to work and run off with some man. I was so incredibly hurt and angry that I did some investigating and managed to find out her new address. Then, one day I got up my courage and went to reclaim my inheritance. I didn't think it would be easy, but in fact everything went so smoothly that it was almost a letdown.

By the time I arrived in the town where she was living, it was late afternoon, almost evening. I didn't try to get into her apartment as soon as I found it because I was afraid she might be living with the sort of man I would rather steer clear of; instead, I decided to spend some time in town, waiting for nightfall.

I'll never forget how I felt then. . . .

The rituals of our daily lives permeate our very bodies. After all we had been through, the one tie that still bound my mother and me was the way time moved in our lives, because it had seeped down so deep inside us.

I wasn't taking the situation that seriously; I even thought the two of us would get together again some day. I knew my mom had let my father's mother take over as my legal guardian, but even so, I still believed we would get back together. I haven't seen her once since she left, though, even today. For all I know, we may never see each other again. Back then it would have hurt me too much to admit that possibility, so I closed my heart to keep from thinking about it.

The town was subject to the same flow of time—the same cycle that had left its mark on my body over the years, ever since I was young. In the evening, around the time the news came on TV, as the birds soared through the western sky, and the huge evening sun hovered in the west, slowly sinking toward the horizon, I had always walked home alone. I might be returning from school or from a boyfriend's house, I might be heading back after skipping school and hanging out all day or even making a special trip back if I was out with friends—as long as I lived with my mom, I always went back in the evening to change clothes.

This was the only time that my mother and I shared. I didn't go back because I wanted to see her—it was a sort of obligation, something I did for her because she had raised me, even though she wasn't related to me by blood. I made a habit out of something that had begun as an instinctive strategy, my childish way of reminding her that I was alive, and that she was supposed to be taking care of me.

My mom was always having dinner when I got home. Then she would leave for the bar. My dad hadn't been home much for a long time; the second half of our life together, my mom and I lived alone. I sat with her for a few minutes while she ate, then saw her off. Bye! See you later! I'd wave goodbye, then go do the dishes and clean up, and then, most of the time, go to a friend's house or to my boyfriend's. I usually didn't come home until very late.

Some nights, my mom wouldn't return. She never brought a man into the apartment, though. My mom had a strict sense of propriety, and the way she saw it, that space belonged to my dad. I was sort of surprised that my dutiful mom ran off with my inheritance, but there's no point going on about that. I suppose she must have hated my father for not leaving her anything after she had worked so desperately hard to raise me.

By the time I'd been to the game center there in that unfamiliar town, and had numerous cups of coffee, and sat on an embankment to watch the sunset, and stood for a while in the bookstore, reading, I was completely and utterly confused.

I seemed to be in some generic town of the sort one encounters in dreams. My heart, bathed in light from the western sun, felt as if it were beginning to rot. My head was spinning; I thought that if I just turned the next corner, I'd be able to get back home. And when I arrived, I'd find those rooms where I had lived with my mom, and the scent of clean laundry would rise up around me, and I would hear the kitchen floorboards creaking—it was impossible not to believe it would all be there unchanged. The building we lived in was fairly nice, but it had been built a good twenty years ago, and in a lot of places it was starting to show signs of age. It was hot in summer, cold in winter. I thought I could go back to that apartment. My mom would be eating dinner as if nothing had happened, and I would burst through the door, and our old life would begin again . . . that's how it felt. Isn't it Monday today? I'll have to fold laundry, I thought, then go do the shopping.

The truth was that my mother was living in an apartment I didn't know, here in this unfamiliar town, with a man I didn't know. When the time seemed more or less right, I made my way back to the building.

My mom always left the curtains open, and they were open now, too, in this new apartment. I had a clear view of her silhouette in the window: she was busy getting ready to go out. The windows were made of frosted glass, but the lights were on, and I could see every movement. After she was dressed, she came back into the room and changed her jacket, just as she used to when we were living together, then looked herself over from head to toe in the full-length mirror by the window—another habit of hers. I became more and more confused, until in the end I no longer had any idea when all this was taking place. If I just walked in there, everything that had happened would be erased——I really felt as if time could run backward. My mom switched off the lights and left the room. Which means, I figured, that the man isn't there.

My mom hurried away, unaware that I was hiding in the shadows. She was a beautiful woman who loved dealing with customers, and she couldn't get along without the pleasures of a job at a bar. She was doing the same work here in this town. Her small back hadn't changed. She walked off at a fast pace.

I quickly checked her mailbox to make sure I had the right apartment number, then slipped my hand through the slot and felt around the top of the box. Just as I expected: the key was stuck there with packing tape, just like always. I took out the key and headed for my mother's new apartment.

The building, which was built on the model of a housing complex, was very big. I was an intruder——my heart thumped each time I passed someone. All kinds of happy noises came through the different windows. The voices of children, of fathers already going in to take a bath, someone calling to someone else, the sounds of dinners being prepared, and the delicious smells . . . I started to feel as if I might cry, so I rushed down the hall very quickly.

My mother's apartment was all the way at the end. I slid the key into the lock and opened the door. Male clothing I didn't recognize hung on the wall. It was a suit. I gave a sigh of relief, because, judging from the style, he was clearly just a regular businessman. She hadn't, it seemed, been sweet-talked by a *yakuza*. My mother was living a new life now. The kitchen looked very tidy; I could smell my mother's scent. There were four rooms. I went into the one where I had seen her silhouette earlier, since it seemed like the best place to start, and opened the drawer where she had always kept her underwear. And just as I expected, my seal and passbook were both there, under the underwear. Looking through the passbook, I saw that my father had left me twenty million yen. She didn't appear to have touched it yet. Taking the money was one thing, but I don't know how she expected me to get along without my official seal. I really needed it. I left the apartment, taking the seal and passbook with me. I locked the door, thinking as I did that it was kind of unusual—a thief locking the door behind her. I had left a slip of paper in the bottom of the drawer on which I had written, in small characters, "Lupin the Third Strikes Again!" though I doubted my amusing *manga* allusion would make her smile. I finished things off by taping the key back where it had been, then caught a train and went home.

The next day I canceled my contract with the phone company and got a cell phone. Then I completed the paperwork necessary for me to move out of my apartment. It would have been a pain if my mother realized the things were gone and came to get the money. I must have used a whole life's worth of energy going through it all. In one sleepless night, I disposed of everything. I packed all my dad's clothes into a single cardboard box. I put his books, his letters, and all the other things he had left behind into storage. None of the things my mother had left mattered—that was why she had left them, after all—so I threw everything away. I also tossed as many of my own things as possible and put the rest into storage with my dad's things. Ultimately, I was able to fit everything into just two suitcases. Two days later, I went to the bank and opened a new account for myself with ten million yen, then had them print up a check for the remaining ten million, which I mailed to my mother. When I got the receipt for sending it by registered mail, an image of the mailbox in that building drifted up before my mind's eye. It occurred to me—and I felt how true it was—that the moment this check slipped into that mailbox, I would really be alone.

I stayed in a business hotel for a while, but then Chizuru suggested that I come stay in her place. She started out as the friend of a friend. I knew she liked me, and I liked her, and at that point in my life I was just looking for a way to buy time until the sense of rootlessness that pervaded my days abated. And so I decided to take advantage of her kind offer.

Living with Chizuru was great, right from the start.

Chizuru saw ghosts, or sometimes sensed their presence. She was the sort of person who would get teary-eyed when something sad happened to a friend, even though she didn't particularly feel like crying. And when my shoulders were stiff or I had gastritis or something, she could make it better just by putting her hand where it hurt. Chizuru explained that when she was a child something terrible had happened to her—she had tumbled down a long flight of stairs—and she'd had these powers ever since then. Her eyes were very clear, and she was always staring someplace a little off to one side of whoever she was with, her gaze full of light. She was a strong person. Nothing scared her.

What's more, her apartment was just the sort of place my troubled heart needed then. It was on the seventh floor of a building that was falling to pieces, right next to the highway, and when you looked down out of the window you saw a bunch of alleys squashed together and a row of slumlike buildings. It was always very loud, many of the tenants were behind on their rent, and the apartment one floor above——a two-room place just like hers——was inhabited by a family of eight that made a stunning amount of noise. Her building reminded me of the slums in Kulong, Hong Kong, which I had seen once on TV.

One day I asked her, So what made you decide to live in a place like this? To which she replied with a smile, Somehow I feel really relaxed here. Because when I see too many ordinary people, I start thinking that I'm strange, and that makes me uneasy.

Chizuru kept things abnormally clean——the floors and the kitchen were always polished until they shone. More than once I'd been awakened in the middle of the night by the sound of her scrubbing the floor, and it was so slick I used to slip and fall all the time.

She almost never slept. She said a few hours of sleep was enough. And that scrubbing the floor was just a way to kill time. She said she had been scrubbing the floors even before we started living together, even though there was no one to notice how clean they were, as she waited for daybreak.

She also insisted that she saw ghosts. She was constantly muttering to herself, saying the most frightening things. There's an old woman coming, and look, she's got a bunch of persimmons! That kid must have been run over by a car, huh? And so on. While I was with her, the world teemed with ghosts.

I had made up my mind that if I couldn't see something, it didn't exist, so I wasn't too concerned about all that. And yet, from time to time, I did sense something. Out on the street, in the apartment. And every time that happened, without fail, she would say someone was there.

In order to sleep peacefully without seeing ghosts, Chizuru always went to bed wearing an array of objects that glowed or lit up. Rings, earrings, bracelets. She said these things kept the ghosts away. As a result, when we had sex—for some reason, she always played a masculine role—I always ended up getting poked in all kinds of places by various accessories, and it invariably hurt.

There really was a lot of fog that year.

When I awoke, near daybreak, Chizuru would

often be sitting with a rag in one hand, partway through scrubbing the floor, gazing out the window.

The headlights of cars would reflect off the fog, filling the air with a mysterious glow. It was like a scene from another world. Or like something you might see at the edge of this world—and that included Chizuru, the spectator. I would open my eyes a crack and watch her, without letting her know I was awake. She would rest her elbow on the rusty window frame, which rattled in the wind, and gaze out like a child, cradling her chin in her hand. The fog out there was milky, so thick it seemed you could reach out and touch it. I felt as if morning might never come. Chizuru's torso and her arms were so thin they seemed to have been rejected by the world. They were only allowed to exist in these peculiar landscapes.

People tend to think they break up because they get tired of the person they've been with— that it's someone's decision, either yours or theirs. But this isn't really true. Periods in our lives end the way seasons change. That's all there is to it. Human willpower can't change that—which means, if you look at it another way, that we might as well enjoy ourselves until that day arrives.

Our life together was peaceful and fun, right to the very end.

Or was I the only one who felt this way? No, I doubt that.

Little by little, as we lived a life fueled by convenience store meals in that old apartment, I began to train my mental muscles, which was what I needed to do to become an adult. It occurred to me that maybe it was time to try living alone. I found a place that was cheap, just right for me, and not too far away; I decided to take it right away, and told Chizuru. She didn't seem particularly disturbed at the time. She just smiled and said, We can still go back and forth, right? So I didn't realize what a shock it gave her.

Our last Sunday together, we felt a little lonely. So Chizuru said she wanted to go for a drive. We headed for a nearby mountain, me behind the wheel of Chizuru's car. We had a lunch of rice with mushrooms at a small Japanese-style teahouse at the top of the mountain, went out to the overlook and stared at the colorful mountains, then went and soaked in a hot spring.

Yes, it was autumn then.

From where we sat in the bath, we had a splendid view of the autumn leaves: foliage brilliant enough to drive you crazy—a kaleidoscope of different reds and yellows. Each time there was a breeze, the leaves danced as if a storm had blown up. We sat for ages in that open-air bath, but the loneliness never went away.

The loneliness of passing time. The loneliness of the fork in the road.

"I wonder why we feel so lonely? It's odd, isn't it?"

We kept repeating such phrases, as if it were someone else's problem.

"Yeah, we'll just be living in different places. What's up with us?"

I felt so bad I envied everyone around us, because they all seemed to be having such fun. All the people who came to soak in the water: the old women, the small children, their mothers. People whose bodies had been molded by the things they did each day, in their ordinary lives. Even after they had all left and new people started coming in, one after another, we stayed there, soaking in the bath. The sky was very high.

"We were inside so much, you know," said Chizuru, "and there was so much fog, and the weather wasn't very nice—it's like a dream, being in such a lovely place."

"Your mind feels sharper, doesn't it? When the sky is clear like this."

Then, in the car on the way back, Chizuru said:

"I'll get out here."

I tried and tried to convince her not to leave, but she insisted. The atmosphere in the car grew heavier and heavier, until finally I couldn't take it anymore, and I let her go. It was almost as if a spell had been cast over me.

When I got back to Chizuru's apartment, alone this time, it hit me. How could you do something like that? But no matter how I looked at it, she had been serious. I decided the only thing I could do now was get out, not wait in the apartment for her to return, so that she wouldn't have to be there when I left. So I packed and cleaned until no trace remained of my existence. I left all the things we had shared. I thought about my life—a life that necessitated two speedy moves in such a short period. And I thought about Chizuru. As fond as I was of her, I wasn't confident that I could love her enough to stay with her, to go on filling the dark, lonely space she carried within her. I knew that someday I would fall in love with a man, and what I would do to her then would be even worse. So I didn't call her.

Then, a month later, once life in the new apartment had finally begun running smoothly on its tracks, I realized that I really did need her as a friend. I made up my mind to go see her at last, and gave her a call.

"Hey, how are you doing?"

Chizuru sounded just the same as always when she answered the phone.

There, in that apartment.

"Sorry I've had the car all this time. Did you get home all right?"

"Yeah, I was fine—we hadn't gone very far. I stayed two nights after you left, and I was able to hitchhike back right away."

"That's good."

My eyes filled with tears.

"I mean, I'm the one who told you to leave me there, right?" said Chizuru, her voice very gentle. "I really did want to stay on, just a little longer—there in the middle of all that nature, that autumn scenery. I wanted to sort out my emotions. I'm the one who made you do it, so I'm not mad at you, not at all. I just couldn't bear to be there when you left."

"I understood how you felt," I said, "but I should have taken you to the station, at least."

"No, it's OK. It's awkward, isn't it? Saying goodbye at a station."

"Yeah, I guess so."

"You know, I had a lot of fun. Living with you, I mean. I never thought I'd be able to live with another person."

"Same here."

"I think you're a really lucky person. I can tell you're going to have a very unusual life. I bet all

kind of things will happen. But you mustn't blame
yourself. You have to live a hard-boiled life, OK?
No matter what happens, keep going around with
your nose in the air."

"What? Do I go around with my nose in the
air?"

"Not really." Chizuru chuckled.

Her voice rang out quietly, like a bell.

"Well, see you around."

"Yeah, see you around."

I felt a surge of relief as I put down the phone.
There might not be any future for us as a couple,
but I began to hope we might come together in
some other way. And I was able to fall asleep—for
the first time since we had said goodbye on that
mountain road, I fell into a deep, deep sleep.

I had a strange dream then, too.

I'm driving back up the mountain, no longer
angry, but in a very gentle mood. In the twilight,
the colors of the foliage fade into each other. I come
to the place where Chizuru and I said goodbye.
Chizuru is there, crouching like a kitten. As I drive
toward her, she smiles happily. She opens the door

and gets in, the expression on her face more vibrant than any I've ever seen. We hold hands. It's hard driving in the mountains with only one hand, but I don't want to let go. Chizuru's cold palm. Her fingers are cold, too, as always. She looks smaller than usual. No matter how dirty her building is, even though the roof leaks when it rains and the walls are so thin you can hear everything, even though there is nothing in the landscape out the window that saves the place, I'm going to go back there with her, and we'll stay together all our lives. . . .

That's when I woke up.

I couldn't begin to describe how I felt.

All day, I kept thinking about that dream. Toward evening, it occurred to me that I hadn't told anyone but Chizuru my new address, so I gave one of my friends a call. He was a mutual acquaintance of Chizuru and mine.

"You're alive!" he shouted. "Talk about the devil's luck!"

"What are you talking about?" I said.

His words resonated strangely with what Chizuru had said earlier.

"You mean you haven't heard? . . . I'm so sorry. The day before yesterday, there was a fire in the building where Chizuru lived. Chizuru died."

"What!" I said, stunned. "But I talked to her on the phone yesterday!"

"That's . . . you know. You know Chizuru. It could happen."

"But how . . ."

"Everyone thought you were still living with her, and we were so worried, we were searching for your body, trying to figure out where you might have gone," said our friend. "We had no way of contacting you or anything—we didn't know what to do. God, I'm so glad you're all right. At least there's something good in this tragedy. I'll tell everyone you're OK."

He wasn't being all that delicate, but I could sense his sadness. I gripped the phone tightly in my hand, overwhelmed.

"Thanks for telling me. Is there going to be a funeral?"

"Some relative came to the hospital—judging

from what I saw, he must have been a pretty distant relative—and went off almost immediately with her body. He said he hadn't seen her in a decade. I guess Chizuru was involved in all kinds of stuff way back when, so her family wouldn't have anything to do with her. I asked the guy to let me know about the funeral and stuff, but he never got in touch."

"Oh. Did you get his number or anything?"

"Yeah, I did. I'll give it to you next time we talk. It would be nice to visit her grave, at least, huh? It's so hard to believe . . . all of a sudden she's just not here, vanished without a trace."

"I know what you mean."

There was one other thing I wanted to ask.

"Did the fire start in Chizuru's apartment?"

"No, it didn't," my friend answered angrily. "It started in the apartment next door, the one where that alcoholic guy lived. Apparently he got completely trashed and left the kettle on the stove. The bastard got out unscathed."

"Oh . . . I see."

I couldn't cry. Even now, I still haven't had a good cry.

I've regretted what I did so many times. I still do. But I keep telling myself not to. *We couldn't have gone on any longer anyway, I know that. And we had fun, right to the end.* Again and again, like an incantation, I repeat these words.

"Oh, that's nice—I wish things were like that for me. What did I do wrong?" the woman said, looking rather put out. I hadn't told her what I was remembering, but she seemed to have read my mind. She looked as if she were truly annoyed, from the very bottom of her heart.

"It's not too late, is it?" I said. "Why don't you go back to your room, maybe talk a bit more seriously about breaking up or carrying on or whatever seems best? And put on some clothes. Aren't you cold?"

"It may be too late," said the woman. Her

hair was covering her face. "We're thinking of committing suicide together. . . ."

She didn't say anything after that. She seemed oddly fidgety.

"Oh my god," I said, "you haven't . . ."

"And what if I did? What if I killed him first, then left the room and came . . . Of course, I'd prefer to think I wouldn't do something like that. Or maybe it was a failed suicide, maybe I woke up, just me, and he was dead. . . . Which one do you suppose it is?" she asked.

"Which one! What are you talking about?" I shouted, Because I had the feeling that unless I shouted, I was about to get very, very frightened. "Forget it, what's the use in talking? I'm going to get the key from the woman!"

I grabbed the key to my room and leapt to my feet. It crossed my mind that if I didn't take my key, I'd fall into the same trap she had. I don't know why. She would still be in my room, after all.

When I looked back, she was sitting on my bed, her feet dangling over the edge, looking lonely.

She kept staring at the ground, without looking up. I noticed how pretty her thighs were, and the V of her collarbone.

I took the elevator down to the front desk and vehemently rang the bell.

No one came out, so I kept ringing it. The only sound was the hum of the air conditioner, which echoed through the dark lobby; the faded colors of the couch seemed to levitate in space.

After an extremely long time, the woman emerged from the back. It was clear that she had just gotten out of bed and she was in a terrible mood.

"A woman staying in a room near mine has a problem—she's been shut out of her room, and she's naked. Do you think I could borrow the key to her room?"

"Huh?" I doubt the human organism can create a voice more foul-tempered than hers was then.

"If you don't believe me, come and see!" I said.

I thought it would be best to have her come, just in case the man happened to be dead or something.

"I'm sorry to say that you're the only guest today!" said the woman.

"What? But, just now, really . . ."

"Oh boy," said the woman. "Which side should I take?"

"What do you mean, which side?"

"Should I think of the hotel's profits or set the customer's mind at ease?"

Her expression was completely serious.

"If you've said that much, you might as well tell me the rest," I said. "What's going on?"

"Listen, I understand what you're saying. This is a strange day. The sort of day when people in the old days talked about seeing sneaky creatures like *mujina*. Somehow the air feels heavy, and the night is darker than usual. But you know what? It will pass. Even nights like this come to an end. Anyway, that woman you're talking about—she was wearing a bathrobe, wasn't she?"

"That's right."

"She appears sometimes. Here in the hotel. A while back, she and her lover planned to commit suicide together here, but she was the only one who died. The man, who was a teacher at the school, survived. There weren't enough sleeping pills. So he took his wife and kids and moved out of town."

"How awful."

I didn't like this at all. But the woman said:

"It's an old hotel, you know. All kinds of things have happened here."

So all I could say was:

"Well, at the very least, no one has really been locked out, and no one's dying in one of the rooms now or anything, right?"

"Exactly," said the woman. "Don't worry, it'll be morning in a few hours. If anything else happens, come wake me up."

With that, she returned to the back room.

I was left standing in the lobby with no choice but to return alone to my room. I would either go listen to more of the ghost's complaints, or I would have another bad dream. The choices were far from appealing.

So I decided to go outside and give my head a rest.

There was an incredible wind blowing outside.

No doubt all the beautiful leaves were falling like crazy right now.

Here, and at the spot where I last saw Chizuru.

I gazed up at the sky, my head full of these thoughts.

The stars were beautiful.

Looking back, I saw that, except for the window of my room and the hall windows, the entire building was dark.

I remembered how lonely the woman had looked.

Suddenly I realized that she had taken most of the pills on purpose.

She hadn't let him take as many as she did.

That's why she seemed so fragile.

I don't know how I knew all this, but I was convinced it was true. What was it about this night that made me so sensitive?

Now that I had cooled off, I went back into the lobby. The woman was awake, standing at the front desk.

"*You're* not a ghost, are you?" I said.

"I'm just a woman who's been working here for a long, long time," she replied. "Thanks to you, I can't get to sleep."

"I'm sorry," I said. "I think I'll go soak in the bath again."

"Be careful. I'll wait up for you—come by when you're done."

Touched by the woman's gentleness, I hurried off toward the bath.

5
The Tatami Room

The springwater that filled the bath was just as hot as before, so I was able to relax and take my time warming my now cool body.

Peering through the glass at the clock in the changing room, I saw that it was almost four.

What kind of night is this? I thought. I encounter something strange on a road in the mountains and end up leading it into my hotel . . . it's too much, it really is. I was reaching the peak of exhaustion then, and the urge to sleep came welling up inside me; my eyes were about to close, all on their own.

This time, no matter what happens, I thought as I gazed at the bath tiles, I am definitely going to sleep.

The tiles were old but the colors were really nice; they made me feel nostalgic. These tiles looked like the ones we had had a very long time ago, when I was small, in the bathroom of the house where I lived with my father and my real mother. Back then, it never occurred to me that my life would turn out like this. I thought I would grow up with my parents the way other only children did, and then go off and get married. Who'd have guessed that I would end up so far away. . . .

I kept gazing down at the tiles, getting a bit sentimental. When I glanced up, I noticed that the rim of the bath was decorated with a simple mosaic made out of ordinary stones.

It's not much of a hotel, I thought, but this is a nice bath. Just then, a shiver ran down my spine. Something inside me had frantically shaken its head.

What was that? This bath is so comfortable, it's nice and small, it has just the right feeling of age, and even the water is good . . . why do I feel this way? I kept mulling it over as I succumbed to another attack of drowsiness, until suddenly my gaze landed on something. . . . In the midst of the grayish stones that rimmed the bath, there was one of a different color—one pitch-black stone, buried among the rest in the mosaic.

So that's what it was!

I felt a strange sense of satisfaction.

This hotel is part of it all.

Somehow one of those stones ended up being used here. That's why all these strange things have been happening.

My heart ached when I thought about what had happened at the *udon* shop, but I decided that since this hotel had been around for ages and was still doing fine, it was probably best to leave things as they were.

True, it might not be appropriate to say the hotel was doing fine, when couples came here to commit suicide and it was haunted and so on. But the fact that no one died at the *udon* shop suggested that the shrine's powers were limited.

I climbed gingerly out of the bath, taking care not to step on the black stone, and then, figuring I might as well, I went back by the front desk.

"Good night!" I called to the woman.

"Why don't you come in and have some tea before you go to sleep?" she said, emerging from the back room. "You don't want to return to your room, do you?"

I was dying to get back to sleep, but I was thirsty, too. I decided to join her.

Going through a door next to the front desk, I entered the back room.

It was a neatly organized, rather small room, with six tatami mats covering the floor. The curtains, which had a floral pattern, were tightly drawn.

The woman stood in the kitchenette waiting for the water to boil.

A vase of brilliantly white chrysanthemums, so huge that they seemed terribly out of place, stood on the table. I wasn't very happy to see them there, considering their funereal associations, but I kept my thoughts to myself, thinking it might be better not to say anything.

The woman must have noticed that I was looking at them, though, because she raised the subject herself when she brought the tea over.

"You want to know about the flowers, right?"

The tea was very hot, and it tasted good.

"It's great. The tea, I mean."

"I've got relatives in Shizuoka, near where they grow it," said the woman. "I was telling you about the flowers, though. Actually, the man who was involved in the attempted double suicide we talked about earlier—he sends them. Every year."

"The one who was going out with the ghost?" I said.

"That's right. They come every year, with a note asking me to put them out as an offering. I can't very well leave them on the front desk, though, can I? Talk about bringing bad luck! That would be about as bad as it gets. On the other hand, I don't like to put them in the room. That's why they're here. I burn a stick of incense in front of them every day."

I remembered the aura of loneliness that had clung to the woman.

"People are always going on about how scared they are of ghosts, but the way I see it, people are much more frightening," said the woman. "You know, I was at the front desk when the two of them came here to die. That sure was scary, let me tell you. It was a night just like tonight, the same strange mood in the air. The man was deathly pale and covered with mud; the woman was barefoot, her hair a huge mess, and she was covered with mud, too. They said they had come over the mountain. They were falling apart, and you could see they were in a very dangerous mood—you know what I mean?—something awful hung in the air around them . . . normally, I would have turned them away then and there, but the woman kept pleading with me, she kept saying, I have to rest. . . . I have to rest. . . . And her eyes were all red and puffy from crying. It was terrifying. . . . So I ended up giving them a room, and then—what a commotion! I just thank my lucky stars I wasn't fired. But you know, she planned it so that only she would die. The pills she took were stronger than the ones she gave him. The man almost went crazy when he heard that. That was when I realized that they had really been in love, it wasn't just a game."

"I knew it. . . ."

"But for her to come back as a ghost . . . I guess that's what people mean when they say no good deed goes unpunished, huh?" said the woman. "Not that it really matters. The hotel will be closing next year."

"Really? This hotel won't be here anymore?" I said.

At the same time, I was thinking, Yeah, well, that's probably for the best.

"That's right. The man who owned it passed away, you see. His son has been saying he might tear it down and build a restaurant in its place next year. You know that bath? The owner built that himself, you know."

"Oh?"

"It's a cute little bath, isn't it?"

"Did he get the stones up on the mountain?" I asked.

"Why?"

"The mosaic is kind of unusual."

"Yes, he was a strange man—he collected stones. I don't mean precious stones like diamonds and things like that. Just plain old stones. Useless rocks."

"I see, I think it's great, though—it's a lovely bath," I said, because it seemed like a nice thing to say. "You should be careful, though. There's a ghost, after all, and there's something funny about this place. Somehow."

"Oh, I'll be fine. I said this earlier, but it's true—you have strange nights no matter where you are. And they always pass. You just have to force yourself to act like nothing is wrong, and when morning comes everything is back to normal. For me, people are the scariest. These other things don't seem like such a big deal, not compared to the gleeful look the owner's son had on his face when his father died. Once, the most elegant couple you can imagine came and took a

room here, and when the man who does the cleaning went in after they left, he saw things so
awful that he vomited. He said he couldn't even
begin to imagine the nauseating things they had
been doing in there. That's the kind of thing that
frightens me."

The woman's tone set my mind at ease.
Everything will be fine, I thought, as long as
they've got someone like her around. I made up my
mind not to worry about the hotel.

"Well, I guess I'll go back upstairs. Good
night," I said.

Outside, there was the faint chirping of a bird.
Dawn was almost here.

"You don't really want to go, do you?" said
the woman. "Why don't you just sleep here?"

"Huh?"

"It's fine, don't worry, there isn't a whole lot
of space but I've got a futon here that you can use.
Trust me, it's better for you to stay. She'll come
back." The woman's voice was bright. "Things
will be fine in the morning—you can go up and get
your bag before you leave."

I don't get it, I thought. I'm paying good money to sleep with an old woman in a Japanese-style room so dull it doesn't even qualify as tastefully restrained. I decided to stay, though, since it was such an unusual experience.

"OK, I will. Thanks."

I was also so tired by then that I didn't care where I slept.

The woman rolled out a futon for me a little apart from her own, which had been spread out on the floor the whole time.

This small room, the low ceiling, the smell of the chrysanthemums.

I got into my futon and said good night.

Good night, replied the woman as she switched off the overhead light.

She was still washing our teacups under the kitchen light, the only one she had left on, when I fell asleep.

6
Another Dream

The dream was very real.

I couldn't even say for sure whether it was a dream or a memory. Though I had the feeling it had actually happened. The dream was extremely short.

I was there, in Chizuru's apartment. In a room that no longer exists.

Everything was so clear; I could even see the stains on the high ceiling.

I saw light glinting off the beautifully polished, stainless steel kitchen counter.

It was foggy outside. So foggy I almost thought it would come inside.

The sky glowed dully and the noise of the traffic was muted.

I could hear the sounds of the couple overhead ardently creating another child in the bathroom, as if they didn't have enough already.

"God, they're so loud!" I moaned. "Don't they know how late it is?"

I was flipping through a magazine; my mind was blank.

Recently, I had become something of an alcoholic; I was almost finished with a two-liter bottle of sake I had been drinking, little by little, and I was very drunk.

"I know, why don't I put on some music?" said Chizuru.

Since she didn't sleep at night, she loved it when I tried to stay up late.

She looked so happy. Just like a child.

Chizuru put on a random CD. It was rather loud, but it still sounded muffled, as if the sound were being absorbed by the fog.

The couple upstairs carried on undisturbed, having such a wild time that every so often we would hear great splashes of water or a big crash as they knocked over the washbasin, or sometimes, in the midst of it all, started discussing their children's education. Everything was so clearly audible that I began to suspect they were doing it with the bathroom window wide open.

"It's amazing. They sure have a lot of stamina. . . ." I said.

To my drunken eyes, Chizuru looked kind of transparent. Maybe it was the color of her skin, or maybe it was the fog, or maybe it was just the sort of person she was. It occurred to me that we might not have much longer together.

For some reason, it seemed natural that a creature like her, who didn't sleep at night and hardly ate a thing, wouldn't live very long.

"Personally, I don't really mind," said Chizuru. She smiled as she listened, entranced, to the mixture of the music and the noises upstairs. "Hearing people makes me feel safe. I don't know, for me, it's kind of a mom-and-dad sound."

"There's a bit too much of the mom-and-dad aspect, don't you think?" I said. "I wouldn't mind if they chose a slightly milder way of expressing it."

Chizuru laughed. "I don't agree. They're all nice warm sounds—the sounds of two parents who went in to take a bath together one night and got to talking about this and that as they washed each other's bodies, and sort of got in the mood."

It didn't matter either way. I was much more interested in looking at Chizuru sitting there by the window, the fog and the glow from the headlights at her back. She looked as if she might vanish then and there. As I gazed at her, I began to feel uneasy, then afraid. Is this our world or the world beyond? I couldn't tell. That must be why Chizuru felt safe when she heard those mom-and-dad sounds—they let her feel that there was something holding her here, on this side.

Everything up to this point was, I'm sure, a mixture of memory and dream.

But then Chizuru turned to face me from outside the window.

"By the way," she said, "I wanted to tell you

that the Chizuru you saw in that dream you had earlier—that wasn't me. This me—the one you're seeing now, in this dream, as you lie sleeping in the woman's room—this is the real me. And you know that shrine you saw earlier? It's nothing to worry about. Really. After today, it won't bother you again. Since I saw that you were in trouble, I kept an eye on you, all along."

Those eyes, they way they looked right through me. Chizuru's eyes.

Tears welled up in my own eyes.

"Thank you," I said, taking her cold hand in mine.

I awoke with a start to find myself in a dark, shabby-looking room that I didn't remember having seen before.

A faint light glimmered through the curtains.

Where the hell am I? I sprang up and saw the woman lying in another part of the room, sound asleep and snoring.

Her hair, which was run through with strands of white, and her nostrils, and those horribly tacky striped pajamas . . . they touched a tender chord in me now. Her receptionist's uniform hung neatly on the wall.

It's people like her, I thought, who keep the world turning.

Feeling a sense of relief, I drifted off to sleep again.

At last this night will end.

7

Morning Light

So morning came. And I went back up to my room.

Bathed in the light of a cloudless morning, it was amazing how peaceful it was. I couldn't imagine what had been so frightening the night before.

I took a shower and got dressed.

Only the two glasses called to mind the events of the previous night, and they didn't seem particularly significant with all this brilliant sunlight streaming into the room.

I quickly packed up my bag and went down to the front desk.

"Thanks for everything," I said.

The woman smiled in reply as she accepted full payment for the room. "Sure, no problem. Take care of yourself."

She acted as if nothing had happened. I chuckled to myself, thinking that this was just about as close to a one-night stand as you could get.

Outside, it was a typical morning in a country town.

One after another the stores were opening for business: gas station attendants went about their work, and an old cleaning lady was sweeping the street.

In the distance, mountains awash with the tints of autumn leaves stood in a line, the blue sky soaring up behind them.

What was all that about last night? I wondered.

Beautiful traces of the final dream still echoed in my heart.

I was glad I'd had a chance to see the real Chizuru in my dream. It could only have happened in that distorted temporality. And it's true, I thought, interesting things do happen, even in the midst of the blackest nights. And when you take a spill, you can always rise up from it with something good in your hand.

I took out my map and began walking toward the station.

HARD LUCK

1
November

For the first time in ages, my mom wasn't at the hospital when I arrived.

Sakai was there all alone; he sat at my sister's bedside, reading a book.

Kuni had all sorts of tubes hooked up to her body, just as she did every day. The awful sound of the respirator filled the quiet space.

I was used to this scene by now, though from time to time I would still see it in my dreams, and somehow the shock I felt on waking was much worse than what I experienced when she was actually lying there before me.

I always felt much deeper emotions when I visited her sickroom in my dreams. In real life, in the train on the way there, I could sense that I was readying myself, little by little. The emotions I would have when I saw her lying there, when I felt her skin, were slowly being pieced together. It was different in dreams. In my dreams, Kuni still talked and walked just like she used to. And yet even in those dreams, I knew it wasn't true. The image of her room in the hospital was always there, somewhere, waiting for me. That scene was always in the back of my mind, always; and so over time the distinction between wakefulness and sleep had faded. No matter where I was, I always felt that something inside me was stretched to the limit, and there was no relief. From the outside, though, I must have seemed very calm. Because as autumn deepened, my face grew less and less expressive, and the tears I cried fell on their own, automatically.

Already a month had passed since my sister had suffered a cerebral hemorrhage. It happened after she stayed up several nights in a row preparing a manual for the person who was going to take over her job when she quit to get married. One cerebral hemisphere was seriously damaged, and the resulting edema put pressure on her brain stem, so that it slowly ceased to function. In the beginning she could still breathe on her own, if only faintly, but eventually her respiratory functions gave out. For the first time, I realized that living on as a vegetable isn't the worst thing that can happen to the comatose. Slowly but surely, my sister's brain was dying.

Recently my whole family had started studying up on these things, and we had learned that my sister could no longer even be called a vegetable— not even that slim ray of hope was left. Just one week ago, we had been informed that her brain stem was functioning at such a low level that her body was only being kept alive by the respirator. My mother had been planning to keep her alive for years, if necessary, as long as she was a vegetable, but now that wouldn't be possible. All we could do was wait for the doctors to declare her officially brain-dead and take her off the respirator.

Slowly everyone in my family came to understand that no miracle would occur, and after that life became somewhat easier. In the beginning, because we had no knowledge to fall back on, we were hounded, again and again, by all sorts of ideas. We lived for a time in a kind of concentrated hell from which there was hardly any escape, torn between everything from superstition and science to our own heartfelt prayers to the gods; we even tried to make out the things Kuni said in our dreams. Then, once we had emerged, sort of, from that agonizing period in which we were constantly assaulted on all sides by conflicting hopes, we calmed down a little and made up our minds to do everything we could to keep my sister comfortable, and not to think or do anything she wouldn't like. By then, we knew that Kuni wouldn't be coming back—and it wasn't just a matter of logic anymore, we could see with our own eyes that it was true. Though when we felt the warmth of her hands or saw that her nails were still growing, or when we heard her forced breathing or the beating of her heart, we couldn't help imagining that something wonderful might happen.

That strange period we all lived through before my sister finally departed from this world forced us all to do a lot of thinking.

That very morning, the day I went to the hospital and found my mother absent, I'd started filling out paperwork again to go and study in Italy—a trip I had been forced to postpone and had been thinking of abandoning all together, depending on how things went with Kuni. We were starting to go on with our lives. Even if every sight that met our eyes was still alive with secret shadows of my sister.

The only one who didn't seem particularly troubled was Sakai, the older brother of Kuni's fiancé. My sister's fiancé had been so traumatized by the terrible thing that had happened to her that he had gone to stay with his mother. As a student in dental school, he knew very well that there was no longer any hope of a recovery now that Kuni's brain stem had stopped functioning. My parents had made a formal request that the engagement be broken off, and the day before he had agreed.

Sakai came to the hospital pretty often, even though none of this had much to do with him—he happened to live in Tokyo, so he said he would like to come if that was OK with us. My family was pretty harsh with him in the beginning because we assumed he was only coming because he was ashamed of the way his useless younger brother was acting. This didn't seem to be the case, though: he came regularly and sometimes tried to hit on the nurses. It didn't seem to have taken very long for him to get used to this devastating state of affairs. I couldn't figure him out.

His life was shrouded in mystery, though my sister had told me at some point that he and his brother had had a hard life. Their father died of some terminal illness, leaving their mother to raise them by herself, working all the while as head nurse in a local hospital. That, as far as I can recall, was the story my sister told me.

Whenever I remembered the time when my sister could still talk, I felt as if there were some sort of membrane around me. My sister had a thin, high-pitched voice, and she talked a lot. When we were kids, we were always dragging our futons into each other's rooms, then talking together until dawn. We swore in the most adorable way that when we grew up, one of us would have to install a skylight in her house so that we could gaze up at the stars while we talked. In our minds, the glass skylight gleamed, shiny and black, and the stars glittered like diamonds, and the air was clear. In that future room, there would be no end to the topics we wanted to discuss, and morning would never come.

My sister was always so cute—there was something about her that reminded you of a fairy tale—but when love was involved she became one very fierce woman, just the opposite of me. When she was a teenager, she was so into her boyfriend that she kept saying she was going to have his initial tattooed on her arm.

"I think it's a bad idea," I told her. "It'll narrow your range of options, right? You won't be able to date anyone later on unless they have the same initial."

"What are you talking about?"

"I mean, say you get a tattoo of the letter *N* for Nakazawa. It won't make any sense if you date someone with no *N* in his name. What happens then? Sure, it'll be just fine if you *happen* to end up with another *N*, but what if you fall in love with someone without any *N*s? You won't be able to explain it."

"I don't see why you're thinking about these things. None of that is relevant! I'll never go out with anyone else! I mean, isn't it romantic to marry the first guy you ever date? I'm pretty sure it's going to work out, you know."

"It's never going to happen. Forget the tattoo."

We enjoyed these silly, late-night conversations, and we had them all the time. Back then our imaginations were so vibrant that, even in the absence of a skylight, we could sense how full of stars the sky was.

At first, the membrane I felt around me when I thought of Kuni would dissolve when I cried, washed away by the hot stream of my tears. But now I had stopped crying. That's how hard I was struggling, body and soul, to accept the situation. I remained enclosed in that membrane—the sense of my sister's absent presence—all the time.

"Where's my mom?" I asked Sakai.

I had left home to live on my own, and now I was in graduate school studying Italian literature. During the past several weeks I had suddenly started doing a lot of part time work, because it occurred to me, after my sister was hospitalized and the possibility arose that she might end up as a vegetable, that I might not be able to rely on my parents for money anymore. I also needed a way to distract myself. My days passed in a cycle of trips to the hospital, time spent with my sister, all-night jobs at bars, going to school, taking naps . . . and I was hardly eating at all. As a result, I learned that all you have to do is change your daily routine, and you start to accumulate an amazing amount of money. It began to seem as if I might even save up enough to cover the cost of my studies in Italy.

With all that going on, I hardly ever went back to my parents' house anymore, though I did keep going to the hospital. I talked to my mother on the phone every day, in addition to seeing her at the hospital. But even so, I couldn't even imagine the depth of her pain. She looked as if she might have some kind of attack herself. Whenever I went to the hospital, she was always there in my sister's room, reading a magazine, washing my sister's thin body, moving her around to prevent bedsores, or talking earnestly with a nurse. Externally she seemed very calm, but you just had to be standing nearby to sense the storm that was raging inside her.

"She said she had a cold or something," Sakai replied.

I found it easy to talk to Sakai, and I generally used informal speech with him, as if he were a close friend my own age, though in fact he was already past forty.

And he had an unusual job. He was a master in a particular school of tai chi with a center of his own where he taught its philosophy and practice. He was the only person I knew who had such a weird occupation. But he had written a book, and he did have students, and I had even heard of people coming from abroad to study with him.

Until recently, I hadn't even realized that people could make something like that into a successful business.

I liked Sakai. I had liked him ever since I first set eyes on him. His unusually long hair, the strange sparkle in his eyes, the difficulty of what he taught, and the unexpected ways he reacted to things—his whole air branded him as an eccentric.

I've always had a soft spot for wackos and oddballs—in fact, my very first love was Tōru, "the boy who swallowed a tadpole in front of everyone"—and Sakai was certainly peculiar enough to intrigue me. Maybe that was why my sister had tried so hard to keep us apart. She was a sharp woman who knew my character well, so she found a way to prevent anything from developing between us. She must have worried a lot, because it really was very hard to know what to make of him. We met for the first time only after my sister was hospitalized.

I was so thoroughly exhausted the first time he came to visit that I was feeling a bit high, and the moment I saw him I thought, *Wow, this guy is awesome!* But since I was so preoccupied with my sister's sickness, I suppressed the feeling. I have always found it relatively easy to keep my emotions in check. I stop being able to savor, even in the secret recesses of my own mind, the ache I feel, and my heart stops dancing when we talk— I convince myself that I never felt anything at all. Kuni always used to say that if I was able to do that, I couldn't really be very deeply in love. *When you're in love,* she once said, *it really hurts, it aches, and you can't suppress it, you want to see it through to the end even if it means that someone has to die, and so you end up causing a whole lot of trouble for everyone.* Judging from the tenor of her comments, I would guess that she was having an affair with someone, probably a married man, at the time.

I used to look at Kuni, envious of the fun she was having. Would she still urge me to fall in love, I thought, even if she was the one who was dying? I always told her that she didn't know what she was talking about, she just fell in love too easily, that was all. Who knows, I said, maybe I'm actually more passionate than you!

But we always enjoyed these differences in our personalities.

I was so carried away by my pain and all the things I had been doing during the past weeks that I forgot how much I had liked Sakai in the beginning.

Now, for the first time since all this had started, my heart had a little room in which to maneuver. Except that ultimately that space was where I would have to learn to leave my sister behind.

"In November the sky always looks so high up, somehow, and it has such a sad, lonely feel to it," said Sakai. "Which month do you like best?"

"November."

"Really? Why?"

"Because the sky is high and lonely, and it makes me feel very alone, and that makes my heart dance, and then I feel stronger. But at the same time, there's this energy in the air; it's a time of waiting, before winter really sets in."

"I know what you mean."

"Yeah . . . I don't know, I just like it a lot."

"As a matter of fact, it's my favorite, too.
Hey, you want a *mikan*?"

"Is it tangerine season already?"

"Come to think of it, it was something else—
some other fruit with a *kan* at the end. I forget what
they're called. Your mom said some relative had
sent them."

"I wonder who? My aunt in Kyushu, maybe?"

"I don't know."

"I'll have one. Where are they?"

"Right here."

Sakai spun around and took a single round
fruit from a basket on top of the TV, a set that was
only there for visitors. Kuni wouldn't be watching TV anymore. She would never again get to see
Nakai, her favorite member of Smap.

"My sister loves these things," I sighed. Every
year she would look forward to eating them—these
fruits that looked kind of like *mikan*.

"Really? Well, then, let's give her one to smell!"

Sakai grabbed another piece of fruit, split it
in two, and held it under my sister's nose. A sweet,

tart aroma wafted through the room, and somehow I found myself watching as a certain scene unfolded before me.

I saw my sister sit up in bed, bathed in afternoon light, and say, with a big smile and in that bell-like voice of hers, "God, what a wonderful smell!"

Of course that didn't really happen—I was daydreaming. My sister lay there with a grim look on her face, making all sorts of noises, fast asleep. But the scene the smell of the *mikan* called to mind seemed so vividly real that I started to cry. It was the first time in ages that I had seen my sister looking that way.

"Did you see it, too?" asked Sakai, ignoring my tears, his eyes widening.

"I think so," I replied. "Do you think that means part of her is actually aware of what's going on around her?"

"No way, not a chance," Sakai said, his tone so definitive that I was taken aback. "That vision we had was brought on by the *mikan*. It brought something back for the two of us, because it remembers Kuni's love."

I started to wonder if Sakai might be crazy.

But he had such a great smile on his face as he went on to say, "The world is a wonderful place, isn't it?!" that something else burst inside me, and I began to sob. I bent over the edge of the bed and wailed as my nose ran and shudders wracked my body. I couldn't stop. I didn't care what it took to make it happen, whether it was a *mikan* or a *ponkan* or something else. I just wanted to see Kuni.

Sakai waited in silence for me to calm down.

"I'm going," I said. "I'm sorry I cried."

"I'm going, too." Sakai got to his feet.

"I don't know," I said. "Kuni might get lonely if you and I both leave at once, and then she'll get jealous."

"All right," Sakai replied, "wait for me downstairs, at the kiosk."

When our eyes met, I noticed something frightening.

He likes me. Oh, so that's it, I thought.

To tell the truth, I was happy.

But we couldn't do anything about it. This

wasn't the right time, and besides, I would be leaving for Italy pretty soon.

The sky was very blue when I went outside. All different kinds of patients and their visitors were gathered around the kiosk.

Somehow none of the patients seemed all that dispirited. Even the ones who were clearly in pretty bad shape were smiling brightly. It was nice and warm in the sun, there were lots of appealing beverages lined up on the counter, and for some reason everyone looked very happy. It struck me that hospitals can be very comforting environments for people who aren't doing too well.

A little later, I saw Sakai heading in my direction.

What would I peg him as, I wondered, just going by how he looks? He doesn't look like a gangster, but then he's not an office worker type, either . . . some kind of entrepreneur, maybe, or—wait, I've got it! He looks like he writes *manga*! Either that or a chiropractor, I guess.

I was still thinking when he reached me.

"Why don't we have a cup of tea before we go?" he asked.

"I'd like a nice strong coffee, actually," I replied.

"There's a good place not too far from here."

"Why don't we walk there, then?"

We began walking.

I felt as if we had been walking around together like this for years. But it was really the first time we had ever been alone together. It felt odd to be leaving the hospital with him, since I would never have gotten to know him if my sister hadn't ended up there. You never know what life will bring. My eyes were so puffy that I couldn't really make out my surroundings. I probably hadn't cried that way, with that same degree of oblivious intensity, since I was a baby.

The sky was distant, perfectly unique, and translucent; the green leaves on the trees were beginning gradually to lose their color.

I thought I detected the sweet scent of dried leaves drifting in the wind.

"I suppose it'll just keep getting colder from now on," I said.

"I guess so. You know, I never tire of the beauty of this season," Sakai said, "no matter how many times I see it."

I wonder when the day will come when he does get tired of it, I thought.

"How do you feel about your brother's behavior, Sakai?" I asked.

"I think he's being just as cowardly as I'd expect—he changes so little that it's actually kind of touching," he replied. "The thing I'm worried about is whether or not he'll actually be able to make it as a dentist and take over the family business. I guess he'll be OK—he's a nice person, after all, and he's good with his hands, and he's pretty sturdily built. I'd be against it if he were going into surgery or something, of course, knowing what a crybaby he is."

A lovely swath of bare branches was visible behind him. It was only November, yet already the branches these trees stretched toward the sky were as bare as bones. I felt safe when I looked into

Sakai's eyes. I saw a light there so deep and force-ful that I felt as if he would forgive anything.

"I always thought he seemed pretty weak myself."

"He is. And since he's so honest, he just ran away from it all. I'm sure he's been crying con-stantly, without even stopping to eat. He'll put his emotions back in order before long, though, and I'm positive he'll be there when your sister dies." Sakai paused. "I know he hasn't come to the hos-pital, and he did agree to break off the engagement, but I can't really blame him for doing either of those things."

"Neither can I. I doubt Kuni does, either."

"Everyone comes to terms with things in his own way, right?"

"It's true. I mean, if you think about it, even I'm starting to make preparations for the future. The way the two of us are acting, your brother and I, isn't all that different, really. I do hope he'll come to the funeral and stuff, though."

"I'm sure he will. You can count on him when it comes to things like that."

"Do you think he might not have left Kuni if her injury had been minor enough that he still could have married her?"

"It's impossible to say for sure, but I doubt he would have. There's something fundamentally different between the hypothetical situation you're describing and what actually happened. The truth is, I think, that Kuni is already saying goodbye to the world—she's going steadily through that process—and in the meantime we're all caught in this odd space, the oddly empty block of time that's left before her death, going through the motions of making a decision. That's how I see it, anyway."

I knew what he meant. The moment I started doing the paperwork for my trip to Italy, the moment I opened my now dusty textbook of conversational Italian and threw myself back into my studies, time, which had ground to a halt, started moving, and I began to feel things again.

It wasn't death that saddened me, it was this mood.

It was the shock of it all.

That stunned feeling remained in the core of my mind, as hard and tight as ever. No matter how hard I tried to make it go away, it never did. Even when I thought I had finally gotten a grip on myself, all I had to do was call up an image of Kuni and all that confidence would disappear.

One morning, Kuni walked into the kitchen clasping her head in her hands.

I just happened to be back visiting my family—I had arrived the night before. I was sitting in the living room, having a cup of coffee.

"Would you like some coffee?" I asked.

"No thanks," she said, her tone strangely gentle. "My head is killing me."

I thought about how Kuni would be getting married soon, and then eventually, when her fiancé was ready to go home and take over the family business, moving to a place much farther away. I started feeling a little sentimental.

It occurred to me that we would never talk about the skylight we used to dream of having, and that our dream would never come true.

Memories of childhood rose up inside me, so vivid that I was dazzled. The air, the different smells, the magazines piled beside our pillows— it all came back to me. Every minute had been fun, I realized, so much fun it made my heart ache.

I went and poked through the cabinet until I found an herbal tea that I'd heard was good for headaches and made a pot for Kuni. She gave me a little smile and washed down two aspirin with a gulp of tea.

I didn't have the slightest premonition of what was going to happen.

If I had, I would have prevented it.

She had on the same pajamas as always and had the same haircut.

I always focus on the present, so why does the passage of time make me so sad? My sister, hope-less romantic dreamer that she was, used to make me go with her at night when she set out to gaze at the window of her first love. As we walked along the darkened streets, we would listen to some song we both liked, playing it again and again, each of us using one earphone from the same Walkman. I wasn't interested in the boy my sister liked, but standing in front of the building where he lived, staring up at the light in his window, was something that made my heart thrill and ache. There were always stars overhead. The asphalt looked much closer when we listened to music while we walked. And the headlights of the cars were beautiful. Sometimes, even though we were still just kids, a guy would try to hit on us, or we would notice someone following us, and we found that electrifying. But as long as we stuck together, nothing could frighten us.

Waves of feeling began surging out, one after another, from the place where they had been dammed up.

Death isn't sad. What hurts is being drowned by these emotions.

I want to run away, I thought—to escape this distant autumn sky.

"What have you done to me, Sakai? I can't stop crying."

"It's not my fault," he said, taking my hand in his as I continued to cry.

The warmth of his palm made me even more emotional.

"Today is your crying day. Go ahead and cry."

"Were you in love with my sister, Sakai?" I asked.

"No," he said. "I only visited her to get closer to you."

I laughed. "Too bad I'm going to Italy, huh."

"It is too bad."

Sakai didn't look like he felt bad, so I wasn't sure what he meant.

"You did know Kuni, though, didn't you?" I asked.

"Sure, I knew her."

"Tell me something about her."

"OK." He agreed right away. "Once, my brother went to a party with a lot of students from other colleges, and he asked a girl there for her phone number. He stuck the slip of paper he wrote it on in his notepad. When he got back to his apartment Kuni was there, and the paper dropped out and fluttered down to the floor, and Kuni kind of sensed what it was, so she tore the whole notepad to pieces right in front of his eyes."

"What kind of story is that?"

"I was staying with him that night, so I saw it happen. I felt this heavy cloud of anger gathering, and I figured they would probably get into an argument later that night, so I put in my earplugs and went to bed early. But it turned out that Kuni was really good at putting things behind her. The two of them went right back to normal after that. Kuni's behavior wasn't forced, and she didn't try to act as if nothing had happened—she just did what she always did. I realized then, for the first time, what a beautiful individual she was. Until then, I had always thought she was just an ordinary woman, and that she was bound to have a pretty frightening temper. Kuni and my brother had this cute conversation after that. What should we have for breakfast? We should get something really good, since your brother is here. Why don't I go get some bread at the bakery that just opened over by the park? Even better, let's go eat there, all three of us! God, it's great to be on vacation,

isn't it? Yeah, really. Things like that. They kept
their voices down so as not to wake me, of course."

"I know what you mean. That's so like Kuni,"
I said, as tears began to trickle from my eyes again.
"God, why am I crying so much today?"

"It's not because you're sad, you know—it's
the shock. The sense of shock you felt at the beginning is coming back for an encore now that the
end is approaching. It takes time, and I doubt
you're going to get used to it, either."

"How come you know all this stuff?"

"Because I understand you," said Sakai.

"Thanks, even if you are just saying that."

If only we could have talked at some other
time, I thought, in other circumstances. Right
now, I need time and I need space. But something
in his easygoing ways made me feel so comfortable
that I couldn't be bothered about those needs.

We walked into the café. It was empty.

We sat down at a table by the window and
sipped our coffee. Everything was very natural,
except for the existence of my sister. She had pene-
trated my world like a dream silently raining

down into my life. And the worst thing was that it didn't bother me at all. I wouldn't have minded if things stayed like this forever. Life was better this way, since the only alternative was a world without her.

"Who can say that Kuni is unhappy, just because she's in that state?" Sakai said. "It's her life and only she can decide. No one else should try. I feel like thinking about that only makes her weaker."

"I agree. I've always been happy because Kuni and I were such good friends. And I'm sure things will never be harder than they are now. My mother doesn't really have a cold, you know—she's just feeling really down. But I know that sometime in the future, a day will come when my family will start to feel differently. That world out there, this landscape we're looking at now, through this window, will start to seem good to us, and different from the way it is now—so different that we aren't even allowed to imagine it yet. It's just that I'm tired of waiting. Because in the early days, I was always waiting for a miracle."

Sakai nodded. "It's natural for you to be tired. Everyone is still stunned by what happened. Even me, as removed from it all as I am. Even the tangerines. We're all stunned that Kuni isn't here anymore."

"Who would have imagined that something like this could happen? And yet right now, even as we speak, similar things are happening all around the world. There are plenty of stories like this in the hospital. I've talked with people about all sorts of problems. They've told me about all kinds of hard choices they've had to make. But until recently, I never even suspected that this world existed."

"That's right. And I'm sure all those people are looking out the window, just like you. But if you turn to face in a different direction, you can get by without having to consider the fact that people like them even exist. Of course, those tragedies and all sorts of other tragedies keep happening whether or not the ones who don't look out the window are aware of their existence."

"Which direction do you face?"

"I think hard about whatever comes before me," he said.

For the first time since all this happened, I really laughed.

Laughing made me forget about everything.

There was a shopping arcade outside, and the strange music that was playing over its loudspeakers drowned out the Mozart playing in the café.

There could be no more affection or hope or miracles now that my sister was getting ready to leave our world behind. Unconscious, her body warm, she gave us time to think. Steeped in that time, I smiled a small smile. There was eternity there, and beauty, and my sister was still with us, the way she was meant to be. Did anyone ever imagine, back in the old days, that eventually a day would come when people and their brains would each die a separate death?

None of this mattered to my sister, who was dying. This was a sacred time set aside for us survivors to think about issues we didn't usually consider.

To focus on the unbearable only marred what was sacred.

And it struck me that if anything was a miracle, it was this: the lovely moments we experienced during the small, almost imperceptible periods of relief. The instant the unbearable pain and the tears faded away, and I saw with my own eyes how vast the workings of the universe were, I would feel my sister's soul.

Sakai understands all that, I thought, and the fondness I felt for him deepened a little more. For me, love is always accompanied by a feeling of surprise. I like people who are always doing things that would never have occurred to me at that moment. As crushed and dispirited as I was, that part of me didn't change.

"It's a perfect November evening—you can smell the end of autumn in the air," said Sakai, looking out the window. "I guess we just have to try and keep our spirits up."

"Keep our spirits up, yes, but not by forcing ourselves to be cheerful."

"Your mom said this morning that if we give

ourselves over completely to our grief, Kuni will only move farther away."

"I'm impressed that she can say something like that so soon."

I had a good view of the branches of the trees that lined the street. Young men and women were looking through clothes at a used-clothing shop; they were having fun, making lots of noise. There was a greengrocer next door with a whole array of different colored vegetables set out under the lights, all of them looking really lovely. Orange persimmon. The brown of burdock root, the orange of carrots. Colors the gods made, so gorgeous one never tires of looking at them.

A month earlier, I never would have believed that I would be feeling so calm again so soon, admiring vegetables while I sat drinking a cup of coffee. One never knows what the future may hold. In our hearts, we were all peacefully saying goodbye to my sister's life. Or rather, we were moving in that direction, because we had no choice. That was the unbending path down which we were headed, as quietly as the deepening of autumn and the onset of winter.

2
Stars

Late one afternoon, I went to the office where Kuni used to work. Total strangers kept coming up to me with tears streaming from their eyes to say one thing or another. After a while it started getting on my nerves, though I felt their pain.

The woman at the next desk began crying when I went through the things in Kuni's desk; she said she couldn't believe how much my hands looked like my sister's. I told her we looked the same naked, too, but she was in no condition to laugh at my joke; she left the office early, still crying.

Everyone wanted to touch me, the way people do at funerals, which made me feel very ill at ease. But I could sympathize with that, too. I learned that Kuni had been a cheerful and dedicated worker, and that she was great with computers. She had been so neat that there was hardly anything for me to get rid of.

I found lots of things in her locker that seemed out of place at the office: a pair of outlandish ski boots, for instance, and all sorts of snowboarding equipment, which she had just gotten into recently.

When the time came to save Kuni's e-mail on a disk and erase all the personal information from her computer's hard drive, even I started to cry. The man who was helping out, one of her coworkers, cried with me. This stranger and I sat in the secretary's office where Kuni had worked, passing tissues back and forth. All these chores made me even sadder than the sight of Kuni hooked up to the respirator, eyes staring into space. I mentioned that to Kuni's coworker, and he said through his tears that he understood. Being with you is agonizing, he said, because it feels like I'm with Kuni. The way you talk, your gestures—it forces me to admit that she's gone, he said. You make me remember her.

I didn't really know much about Kuni's day-to-day life. Just that she worked as a secretary for one of the company's directors.

But there at the office, I realized that the loss of one ordinary worker is enough to send emotions rippling through the entire staff of a company. And the traces of that emotion would never disappear. I understood then that I couldn't just give up on the world. It would have been easier if I were the kind of person who could simply blame the company for Kuni's death, but I knew that she and her own bad luck were the real culprits, so I couldn't try to put the blame anywhere else. And so I was left with nothing but an inward glow, a trace of the tiny, respectful, adorable light she had given off. No doubt she had worked herself so hard, both mentally and physically, because she didn't want to cause problems for the people she loved. No one was to blame. Life in a company is hard: when you're working frantically to prepare things for your successor, no one tells you to go home and take it easy, because if you don't you might have a cerebral hemorrhage.

Kuni's coworker and I both had red eyes by the time we finished what we'd been doing. Around then, my dad arrived. He went in to greet my sister's boss and the company president.

After my dad and I said goodbye to everyone, a big crowd of people helped us carry my sister's things down to the underground garage. All these nice men and women in their suits, people I'd never meet again. Somehow we managed to pack everything into the car, and I waved goodbye. It was the first time I had met most of these people, and yet for some reason I had the illusion that I was the one who had been working there, and I was quitting my job to get married, and the things we were taking with us were my own.

"Why did you come in the small car, Dad?" I said after the car started moving. "Didn't I ask you to bring the station wagon?"

"Your mother took the wagon to the hospital," said my dad. "She's so worn out that she can't think straight anymore. I suppose it didn't even occur to her that she didn't need the big car; she just got in the wagon and drove off. So when I went out to the lot to get the car, this was the only one there. What was I supposed to do?"

There were so many of my sister's things in the car that I ended up sitting in a very peculiar position, scrunched up in the passenger seat.

The streetlights seemed strangely close from this angle, and they were very pretty. And I could see lots of stars. I felt sick to my stomach, but I thought I could put up with the discomfort if it was just for a short time, because it made the world seem kind of new.

"It doesn't matter."

"I wish you wouldn't talk to me from down there," said my dad.

"I can't help it, can I? Can I lay my head on your lap?"

"Sure."

"I feel like a kid again," I said. My dad's thighs felt just as hard as they had when I was little. "Yes, a young, beautiful woman is resting her head on your lap, it's true, but I don't want you getting excited and having an erection, OK?"

"Why would you make such a vulgar joke about your own father?" asked my dad.

The stars were beautiful. The streets kept whizzing by.

"Apparently they're going to take your sister off the respirator soon."

There was no difference between my dad's tone when he said this and when he'd said "Pooch is dead" when the dog we had had for so long and who had liked my father best passed away. That's how deep his sorrow was.

"God, how could this have happened?" said my dad. "It's like a bad dream."

Like a bad dream.

"It really is a bad dream," I said.

We lapsed into silence. I inhaled the scent of my father's pants.

Unfortunately the car also smelled of my sister's perfume, the scent of which hovered over all her possessions.

Maybe I'll switch to this perfume, I thought. Because it made me feel as if my sister were riding in the backseat, and I really did feel like a child again.

Back in the days when our family went on drives.

The Guerlain perfume my precocious sister had used even in her teens.

"Are you going out with that guy?" my dad asked.

The suddenness of it jolted me back into reality.

"What guy? You mean that fat guy at the office, the one I was crying with?"

"No, not him," said my father. "The weird brother."

"Sakai? Our relationship isn't at all like that," I said. "And you shouldn't say things like that. He's a really nice person, you know."

"Maybe, but if you were to marry him or something, that spineless brother of his would be a relative, and then he'd come see us again, right?

I can't stand the thought of that. Just thinking about it makes me angry."

"I doubt he would come. Besides, Sakai and I really aren't going out or anything. He's a great guy, though. I think so, anyway. At any rate, I know it's hard not to bad-mouth his brother, but Kuni did fall in love with him, after all. Let's try not to say nasty things about him."

"I didn't really mean it. But what's he thinking, going off to his parents' house like that? It's not a joke, you know? He must have been crazy if he thought he could marry my daughter if that's all the feeling he has for her."

Realizing that my father needed a bad guy right now, I gave up defending him. I didn't have much of a sense of what my sister's former fiancé was like. All I knew was that she loved him, and she had gotten as swept up in her love as she always did.

"We should be glad she didn't marry someone so flaky," I said.

"What is there to be glad about now!" shouted my dad.

"I didn't mean it," I said.

"God, it hurts. It really hurts."

My father's voice came from deep down in his belly, and I was feeling carsick; the combination of my queasiness and his pain made me start crying again. The tears I shed lately, particularly those linked to memories, were all but meaningless. They came out on their own, like bird shit. My dad knew this, and kept quiet.

The town where I was born and raised kept whizzing by.

"Mom isn't doing too well, is she?" I said. "Maybe I'll stay at home tonight. I want to go through Kuni's things, anyway."

"Yes, you should stay," said my father. "She'd like that."

"OK. I'll make something for dinner, then."

"How about a hot pot or something? I'd like something hot."

"Sure, if you can stop by the store."

Just then, as we were talking in the warm car, it hit me: we were having a good time again.

Kuni hadn't only given us pain, she had also

created moments for us that were so much more concentrated than usual. That's how I saw it then. In the world we now lived in, the good times were a hundred times better. If we couldn't catch that sparkle, only the agony would remain. Each new day was a struggle, in both the positive and the negative senses. I didn't want my mind to be muddled when the time came to say goodbye to my sister.

3
Music

A few days later, Kuni was taken off the respirator. We all confirmed together that she was dead.

It said in a book that my sister's brain had dissolved. But from the outside, her face looked exactly the same: Kuni's face. After we did her makeup, she seemed even more alive. She looked as if she were about to leave for work. I brushed my finger across the foundation in her compact. Kuni always kept everything so clean—the mirror was spotless, and the sponge. I felt her life in everything. We dressed her in her favorite clothes and filled the coffin with her favorite flowers.

My sister's face was lovely when they carried her off to the crematory.

I had wanted my mind to be clear when this time came, but of course I was in a daze the whole time. I felt as if my eyes weren't focusing, because they didn't want to see what was happening. And that really made me feel lost, as if I were swimming in a dream world. My head was reeling the whole time; I just had to get through each new thing that happened as quickly as possible. My mom only stayed in bed for one day.

Sakai wasn't there for my sister's last moments, of course, but his brother was. Even with my dad punching him and my mom wailing at him, he stayed and saw my sister through the last hours of her life, and then helped out with the funeral. His tenacity then was splendid. If it were me, just getting looks like the ones my parents were giving him would have been enough to send me running back home. I had a chance to talk with him for a little while. He wasn't a bad guy. If things had happened the way they were supposed to, I would have been seeing a lot of him from now on, and we could have taken our time getting to know each other over the years. Now, after a single conversation at this sad event, I was unlikely ever to see him again. It's so strange—the ties that bind us to people. But I know Kuni was glad he came. After all, she was a woman who lived in love.

I was lonely now that Kuni had officially died and I couldn't go see her any more.

Sometimes I would burst out sobbing. One evening when I was taking a bath, for instance, I noticed that the Bulgari animal soap she had brought back for me as a souvenir of a trip overseas had lost its animal shape, even though it had seemed like it would last forever, and was now just a round blob.

Time passes.

Actually, time had always been passing. I had just managed to avoid thinking about it very much. It would be hard for me to recapture that feeling—life wasn't so easy anymore. Small things pricked my heart. In those early days, I lived in a world of overwhelming sensations; it was like I had just fallen out of love.

I realized again how much I wanted to see my sister in the flesh, even the way she looked when she was dying. Because back when she was still in the hospital, I had been able to take that soap down and use it without giving it a second thought.

I made a lot of progress in Italian, because I had nothing else to do.

Later on, there would be my life in Italy. I would stay in touch with my mom and dad and be a support for them while I was gone. And I would throw myself wholeheartedly into whatever I did, so that I could get a good job. It would take a tremendous amount of energy to get my interrupted life back on track, whether it ended up being a twisted version of my old life or a life in which I gained something despite the loss of my sister. I also would never forget that now I was the only child my parents had.

*

I saw Sakai two more times: once on the day of the funeral, then again on the evening of the following Sunday. Somehow evening seemed like the best time to get together with him.

I had been dashing about in my mourning clothes, making arrangements to have boxed lunches distributed to the guests; when I saw Sakai, I heaved a sigh of relief. Just knowing that there was someone in the temple who could take care of himself, whose feelings didn't need to concern me right then, just knowing that his vibrant light was shining there made me breathe a little easier. I hurried toward him, smiling.

"Can we get together one day soon?" he asked.

I smiled. "This is hardly the right occasion to ask me that."

"How about Sunday? Are you free Sunday?"

"Yes, I think so."

We agreed on a time and place. The temple was flooded with afternoon light, and the mood was peaceful. Sakai said he was going for a walk, and disappeared among the graves.

The sky was that ambiguous color peculiar to Tokyo: very faint traces of white seemed to have been mixed into the blue. The trees among the gravestones looked cold and barren. The guests all had on black coats; they were like crows wheeling around the temple. I didn't feel cold. I felt relaxed now because Sakai was there. I had never felt such a sense of complete reliance on someone—on the very fact of his existence, the knowledge that he was alive. I felt like a little bird gazing up at the sky from her nest. I knew he was weird, and kind of a fraud, and that he was cold and unreasonably cheerful, and that he had no sense of responsibility. But none of that mattered. I could rest my wings in that endless expanse. And that was enough. Maybe that's all our relationship was. Right now and forever.

After Kuni died, I ate nothing but curry—her favorite food.

So naturally Sakai and I went for curry, too.

The restaurant was kind of strange: you sat right on the floor, and the curry you got was Indian, not the Japanese-style curry most places serve. People stared as they walked past the window. We concentrated on our curry, sweating.

"Do you have a girlfriend, Sakai?" I asked.

"No, not really," he said. "Just girls who are friends."

"I wonder if we'll ever get together like this again," I said.

"I'm sure we will. And it won't be too long, either."

"The timing is so bad . . . it's hard to think right now."

"I'd be surprised if you suggested that we start dating right now."

"I talked to your brother at the funeral, you know. Quite a lot."

"I bet he was really weak."

"Yeah, he was crying the whole time."

"You know . . . I really hate it when people talk like experts about things they've never experienced, so I don't want to say much about all this. I'm sorry. Actually, I once lost someone close to me. But it didn't happen like it did with your sister, and I've never been a parent. So I have a hard time imagining what it's like, even for my own brother. And for Kuni, of course. And for you. I don't understand how it feels, but even so I think I kind of get what's happening, just from what I've seen and heard, and what I've felt. There are so many things I want to say to you. But I can't say them—they just won't come out."

Sakai said all this in a very formal tone.

"Not many people *have* experienced this sort of thing," I said, smiling. "And I don't particularly want people to understand, anyway. I realize how good you've been to me, though."

When we went outside, the winter sky was full of stars.

"There was a passage in a book I read a long time ago," Sakai said, "about how if you hear extraordinarily beautiful music on a street corner, it means that the same piece will be playing for you when you die. The main character is walking down the street one fine afternoon when this incredibly lovely melody starts coming from a record store across the street. So he sits down to listen. His spiritual guide tells him this is a sign that destiny has put before him, a sign that shows death is present in every aspect of people's lives. And the spiritual guide says that when the man leaves the world, he'll hear the incomparably beautiful tone of that trumpet once more."

"Hey, the same thing happened to me!" I said. "One winter afternoon I was in the place we've just come from, the curry restaurant. I was having a *chai*, all alone. They had the radio tuned to this station that only played reggae, so there were all these minor reggae songs playing, tunes I'd never even heard of, one after another. And one of them came into my head so clearly it felt like a bolt of lightning hit me. It was a duet with a man and a woman singing, and it was about summer vacation. It was a pretty dumb song, nothing special; the thing is, it came straight into my head. And even though it was winter, my mind became full of sunshine. And suddenly I knew: I'm going to die on a summer afternoon. I was so sure of it. Of course, I can't be sure it will really turn out that way."

"You know, I bet that's exactly what it's like."

"I wonder what Kuni's last song was," I said.

A chilly wind gusted down the street. We were walking through a residential area with very few people around; we were going to keep walking until we came to a place where we could get some tea. I wished the street would never end.

"I wouldn't know what the song was either way, but doesn't it depend on when she died? Was it when she lost consciousness? When her brain was damaged? Or did it happen when her brain died? Or when they took her off the respirator?" Sakai paused. "I guess we'll find that out for ourselves sooner or later."

These were hard words, but when he said them it didn't anger me at all.

The trees on either side of the road stretched their bare branches over our heads, creating a tunnel of black silhouettes. I took out my MD player as we walked.

"There were only two tracks on the mix my sister was making before she died. I've been listening to them a lot. I mean, not that this is really related to what we were talking about before."

"What songs are they?"

"'September' by Earth Wind & Fire and Yūmin's 'Autumn Travels.'"

"What a pair! Was it an autumn theme or something?"

"I think that must have been it. I mean, I can see why the Yūmin song is there: Kuni was such a devoted fan of hers that she was actually hoping that her marriage to Matsutōya Masataka would fail."

"Wow. You can tell her age from those songs, though."

"Why don't I put them on while we walk?" I said.

We listened to the songs, each of us using one earphone, the way Kuni and I did back in the old days. These songs had seen my sister through the last September of her life. They weren't selected for that role, it just happened that way. If Kuni had lived, she would have kept editing the minidisc, adding songs, playing it in the car. She had spent her last September, her final days, gazing up into a distant sky that still bore traces of summer. By November, Kuni was gone.

"Come to think of it," said Sakai, almost shouting, "my brother sings this song a lot when we go to do karaoke."

"He sings 'September'?"

"Yeah."

"That's pretty weird. But that explains why it's on the disc."

"Right, that must be it."

"Is he good?"

"My brother doing Earth Wind & Fire, all on his own? Yeah, he's good, but it's scary as hell."

"Oh."

We kept walking, singing along with the music. Do you remember, we crooned, our voices light, the twenty-first night of September? And as the music reverberated in our ears, the road zoomed closer and the sky seemed to widen. I felt as if the world had grown a little more beautiful than it was before; all of a sudden the cold and the darkness of the night were transformed into a lovely splash of light. I realized that my feet were hitting the ground in time with the beating of my heart. And I felt as if the world where I had walked with my sister when we were kids was living again. I felt a rush of nostalgia. This feeling I have right now, I thought, this is what first pushed me into the world, what helped me grow up to be what I am.

The second song—Yūmin's incredibly depressing "Autumn Travels," which, for reasons I can't fathom, was Kuni's favorite—started playing.

And then Sakai spoke.

"I know that right now your heart is still reeling from the shock, and it feels like the middle of winter. But if I go to Italy to visit you when summer comes, will you take me around some towns out in the country?"

"Of course!" I said.

"It's not like we're out of luck, is it? We're just too wrapped up in this mood, right? It wouldn't work out now. But that's because the timing is bad, right?"

"I think so."

The image of those tubes, the sound of the respirator, and the painful light that streamed through the window were still etched into our memories.

"We'll go out every afternoon for pasta, and the sky will be clear, and we'll go see all kinds of scenery. We'll walk until our feet hurt, and drink wine, and we'll sleep in the same room. We'll look out new windows, and feel different from the way we do now with all that summer light pouring down around us, when it's so hot we can't stand it. I'll wait until then——I won't forget you. I don't want things to end like this, only having known you during this strange time. But right now, I just can't think about the future."

Sakai nodded. "I know."

The music kept ringing in my ears. The winter stars were always there, always the same when I turned my gaze upward, no matter who I was with. It was me who changed. The three stars in Orion's belt were still there, just the same. Just as

they had been in the days when Kuni and I raced
to find them first.

   . . . Yes, it will happen just like it does in the
lyrics of Yūmin's song, I thought. This autumn
will never come back; it was one of a kind. And
it's setting out on its distant travels tonight,
weaving away through the barren winter trees.
And then, ever so quietly, a cruel, unknown winter will set in.